Sweet Engla

Sweet England

STEVE WEINER

Vancouver
New Star Books
2010

NEW STAR BOOKS LTD.
107 – 3477 Commercial Street | Vancouver, BC V5N 4E8 CANADA
1574 Gulf Road, #1517 | Point Roberts, WA 98281 USA
www.NewStarBooks.com | info@NewStarBooks.com

The publisher acknowledges the financial support of the Canada Council, the Government of Canada through the Book Publishing Industry Development Program, the British Columbia Arts Council, and the Government of British Columbia through the Book Publishing Tax Credit.

Cover design by Mutasis.com
Illustration by The Quay Brothers
Printed and bound in Canada by Imprimerie Gauvin, Gatineau, QC
Printed on 100% post-consumer recycled paper
First printing, November 2010

LIBRARY AND ARCHIVES CANADA CATALOGUING IN PUBLICATION

Weiner, Steve, 1947–
Sweet England / Steve Weiner.

ISBN 978-1-55420-055-9

I. Title.

PS8595.E4198S84 2010 C813'.54 C2010–905231–5

Dedicated to the memory of Ewan MacColl

In this great orchestra devoted to the worship
of appearances, each has his turn to beat
the drum of existence.

HAKIM NURUDDIN ABDURRAHMAN JAMI,
15th century, *Yusuf and Zulaikha*
translated by David Pendlebury

A flint and stone church stood on a grassy rise in Somerset County, England. Its red door was broken.

Inside, old wall paintings, red and brown, mixed with stains that trailed where rain had fallen. A lavender carpet lay rolled in a corner. There was no roof. There were no pews. Walls had buckled and were now reinforced with iron S-shaped brackets. The rear rosette window was cracked. Mottled wax was hardened on an altar's dirty linen. Nails lay in a heap. Steps led down to a wood crypt door studded with black bolts, locked with a silver chain.

A man in a black coat turned around three times. A bird flew low, one wing up, one wing down, through the nave past his shoulder.

"O!"

A horse came into the church nibbling a radish.

"O —"

He went out.

"Sun!"

It smelled of sweet hay. A barley mow rotated through the rye. To the north, a shaggy head on a pole moved its mouth. The sun's aureole flared between the lips. Far beyond, fishermen pulled a boat on wheels up a winding cliff road to save a life in a sparkling sea.

He ate a garlic growing at the graveyard wall.

"Garlic . . ."

The wall was hot. Grasshoppers clung to thistles where fallen cox apples had crumpled and browned. A long-legged spider stepped over terra cotta shards. A mantis stood on Queen Anne's lace. Tombstones leaned. *The Minister's Grave By Anonymous Hands to Heaven Conveyed. In Service of a Foreign Mission.* There was a low rusted iron braided rail. *Children, Rise and Call. Who Was Awakened Into Life.* A ring of black iron bells lay among shattered urns. A broken slab leaned on itself. *Do Not Judge Love Is Love.*

Dust settled on his coat.

"Dust . . ."

The man climbed into the barley. Far below, in the Avon Valley, a fast train rocketed past sun-struck saplings that bent away under an aqueduct basin with white stone balustrades. A green and white canal narrowboat, *Sweet England*, glided out from a leafy hillside on brown and green water into the sun. Azaleas bloomed at a lock-master's house. A boy in a red vest leaned on a wood lock lever.

A road radiated.

"O."

The man walked the road to a village's first crossroad where a cross of bark and twigs was covered by a bark roof. He walked the lanes. Narrow stone houses had steep gabled and blank windows, stone-ledged. A stone market hall was in the market square, with chipped pediment and a sagging lintel. A green iron gate had green bars with green teeth. Light flitted on potatoes, chamomile, dill and thyme in wicker baskets.

Men with blank eyes wore fingerless gloves.

They mouthed

Pears!

Chamomile!

Potatoes, luv!

A fat man wiped a lamb's mouth. An old woman bent over and tied a wheat sheaf to her backside.

Sweet almonds!

Butchers chopped meat by smoking pots. They milked hens and emptied pigs' bladders into pots of boiling oil. Sausages were split open.

Ow!

Bulls on hooks winked.

Pain!

A boy lifted a sheep's tail and blew into its rear.

"Baa-aa-aa!"

Dancers came to the market square. In tall hats and knee-length breeches, right arm down, left arm up, they hopped on silver-buckled shoes. One man wore antlers and bells on leather anklets. Two men's heels turned to toes and toes to heels so that suddenly they danced backward.

The sun began to go down. The man walked a blue tarmac road through saffron fields.

A Romany wagon leaned against a birch. Clouds turned rose. The long English night turned cobalt. Pink-edged clouds moved over a lake and a castellated church. A boy led cattle home, lanterns swinging from every horn. A mist moved in an orchard. Girls wearing wide-brimmed hats plucked apples. They climbed ladders and put their apples one by one into their baskets.

They sang:

Shall we pass this way again O no never.

The road became ruts, then only brown pine needles in a woods. The man went deeper. A bird thrashed in the cleft of a stump. Cabbages oozed. Wet mud gleamed. It smelled of decay. At the edge of a bog a red concertina opened where pink dragonflies clung to ferns. An ear trumpet sank. White hands dripped milk. Little Lambkin tip-toed on lily-pads, carrying a bleeding cradle.

A pub lighted up.

"O."

It had a sway-back roof spine, bulging pink walls with cracked black timbers. Moths circled a street lamp covered with white climbing roses. Its pub sign hung still. *The Bosom of Abraham.* Red lamps burned in thick amber windows. He went in. It was warm and filled with the fragrance of a wood fire. Ales, gins, vodkas and whiskeys flickered behind red tin coffeepots stencilled with daisies at the bar.

The bar was varnished wood, posts and a wood canopy. Brass horseshoes lined the rafters and a horse collar hung from a nail. A hunting horn, a drenching horn and a black balling iron hung from nails on both sides of a painting of a blue castle. Horse twitchers hung next to a tooth rasp and a singeing lamp. A drum and red regimental flag stood by a fireplace.

"What'll it be," the publican said.

"Local ale."

"Good choice."

The publican pulled a white ceramic and brass handle. Ale filled a glass.

"You've come a long way," he said. "You're in the Home Counties now. Did you know that?"

"No."

The man counted his change.

"I've old money," he said.

"Old?"

"Terribly sorry."

The publican paused.

"I see."

An old man cutting corks waved his knife.

"I'll pay," the old man said.

"Thank you, sir."

The man took his ale.

"What's your name?" the publican said.

"Not sure, really."

"Mind if I call you Jack?"

"No."

"Jack Russell," the publican said. "You look like a dog."

Jack Russell took his ale to a table at a black window where a ceramic fishing boy sat next to a ceramic cow holding dried red strawflowers. He drank. A fiddler played. A man step-danced on a sixteen-inch dance board. He held a full pint of lager.

"Not a drop! I didn't spill a drop!"

The fiddler left. A man in a checkered shirt, a barrel chest, sat backwards on a chair, rolled up his sleeves and sang, one hand to his ear.

I'm a rover and seldom sober
I'm a rover of high degree
It's when I'm drinking I'm always thinking
How to gain my love's company

The publican pointed to Jack's glass.

"Another?"

"Cheers."

The publican's arm elongated across the room, took the empty glass and left a full pint. Jack drank it. The publican rang a bell.

"Time!"

Jack got up.

"Shall I go now?" he said.

"Yes."

The publican took Jack outside.

"A gate is open for you," he said. "Take it — don't mind the owner — he's an eccentric — and follow through a maze to London."

"Will do."

The *Bosom of Abraham* disappeared. The sky was black. Jack walked down the road to an open black gate with gold flourishes. It led to a creek choked with glossy black bushes and reeds. An egret stood on one leg. THE THROWING OF LIVE OR DEAD ANIMALS INTO THE

WATER IS PROHIBITED. A Land Rover drove up. The driver jumped out. He wore black rubber boots and a bell around his neck. He waded into the reeds, took out a knife and cut stems from old roots.

"Did you hear me?"

"No."

"No, you didn't. I didn't say anything. People like you don't listen. Look. Watch me and learn. We English coppice the woodland. England is managed. A natural wood doesn't last. Open water, then tall reeds grow at the fringe, fill in, make a bed, seven kinds of willows. They all collapse."

He got on his hands and knees.

"O, England!"

He chewed swamp cabbage.

"Sweet England!"

He got back into the Land Rover and pointed to a dark tower on a hill.

"See that folly? I built it! I haven't wasted my life!"

The Land Rover drove off.

Jack walked down an allée of pollarded trees past a Temple of Music and a grove of monkey pod trees. Sweet William lined a serpentine path cut into a spongy lawn. Egyptian sphinxes crouched on rain-melded pedestals. Pocked stone spheres gleamed on columns.

A villa glowed.

"O."

Classical statues of women led to a cupola with black slits. Stone beasts climbed stairs. Pale chimneys at roof corners were studded with stony knobs. An orangerie with tall black windows had a maroon ceiling, four burning electric lights and a black and white marble floor. An alabaster coffin on a catafalque was carved with angels. Above, men in white straight-jackets hung from cords tied to their wrists behind their backs. A fencing instructor paced the floor and slashed the air with a rapier.

They turned to Jack.

"Remember us!"

A maze led to a tunnel. A train bleated. *British Rail apologise as somebody has thrown himself on the track between Chalk Farm and Belsize Park. A police investigation is required before we recommence running on the Northern Line.* It was day. It rained. Black taxis splashed past Lebanese restaurants. Clouds rolled over north London. A man in a pink shirt waited on the corner of Agincourt and Mansfield Roads.

"Are you Jack?"

"Yes."

"I am Mr. Salmon. Your landlord. Come see the flat."

Mr. Salmon opened an ochre picket gate. A concrete walk led to a recessed door between two slender pillars. There was a stained frieze. A low bay window hung over a pebbled yard.

Mr. Salmon unlocked the door.

"In."

Jack went in.

"Light!"

Mr. Salmon flicked on the lobby switch. A low amber bulb barely glowed over a small brown carpet flecked with sawdust. Green vinyl chairs were stacked against a white door with a skeleton key from which a string hung. They went up stairs partly covered by a thin runner carpet. Dust circled in light shafts. *Mr. Salmon is an enemy of the working class.* A mattress leaned against a wall. Loops of white rope hung from the landing. *Foreigners go home. English go home.*

Mr. Salmon unlocked a landing door.

"In."

Jack went in.

"Fully furnished!"

A blue couch stood at a bay window.

"A suburban villa out of the pattern book!" Mr. Salmon said. "Gorgeous! The prospect!"

Outside, across the road, a long white building with slab balconies stood behind regularly planted trees on a strip of lawn.

"That's Waxham House," Mr. Salmon said. "Part of the Gospel Oak estates."

"Gospel Oak . . ."

"Yes. *The Oak* marks the actual spot. O! The kitchen!"

They went to the kitchen,

A wood platform with posts, brass hooks and a velvet cord rose from a red floor. A white cooker and basin were next to a narrow window, half of which had a white lace curtain. It also looked out onto Waxham House. They went back to the living room.

"Contemporary design," Mr. Salmon said.

"Contemporary?"

"It was."

Jack leaned out the bay window.

"What parish am I in?" he said.

"St. Pancras."

A low white building was partly hidden behind a wooded playground.

"That's The Beacon," Mr. Salmon said. "Charismatic Christians. Used to be owned by the Moravian Brethren."

"Do they sing?"

"The Moravians?"

"The charismatics."

"O, yes!"

Mr. Salmon paced the floor. His pink shirt was sweaty and his black tie askew. His black trousers were crisp but his black shoes were dusty.

"Can you see better?" he said.

"Yes."

"Belief will do that."

Outside, a man entered a narrow black gate and went up to a walk over allotments.

"The bedroom!"

They crossed the living room to beads hanging in a doorway.

"The place!" Mr. Salmon said, nudging Jack.

"Eh?"

"Don't be shy."

Jack went in. Wicker wagon-wheels were the headboard for a double bed covered with a leopard-skin duvet, under a long mirror on the ceiling. Floral pink globes were in silver sconces. A dead fuchsia drooped on a night table. A black blazer with silver lapels hung in a closet. There was a dresser with stubby legs. Around a corner the bathroom had black and white tiles, a combination bath tub and shower and a black diamond-rimmed medicine cabinet with a mirror.

"Shouldn't the door open outwardly?" Jack said.

"No. Inwardly."

Three chrome cylinders held toilet paper.

For those for whom sin is a possibility
For those for whom sin is a probability
For those for whom sin is a certainty

Jack brushed his hair with his hands. He blinked.

"Did you bruise me, Mr. Salmon?"

"No."

"Somebody did."

Mr. Salmon left. It was night. There was a knock at the door. Jack opened it. A tubby woman with tufted black hair, her face sweaty and green eye make-up smeared, sat on the threshold, her back to the flat. She was drunk.

"I am Brenda."

She fell backward into the flat. Her head bounced.

"Your assignment."

Light fluttered over her haunch. Jack closed the shade on Gospel Oak and hauled her through the beads onto the bed. They writhed. Their images in the ceiling mirror split and came round again. A train bellowed through Gospel Oak. The fuchsia bloomed. Red silhouettes tiptoed through the flat, recoiled in horror.

"O!"

"O!"

Brenda elongated.

"Gor blimey!" Jack said.

"EH?"

"GOD BLIND ME!"

Jack fell off the bed and crab-crawled to the living room.

"THE SHOCK!"

A black bladder leaked. Sparks flew from his hair. Brenda came wearily through the beads, bow-legged, holding the leopard-skin duvet. Her ears were wrapped around her head and tied in a bow. Her nose was bulbous, purple.

"We're caricatures," she said.

"What?"

"OUR LOVE HAS MADE US CARICATURES!"

It was dawn. Brenda opened the curtains. There was a billboard. *Leverton & Sons Ltd. Independent Funeral Directors since 1789 Finchley Road Golders Green also at Hampstead. We recommend a pre-paid funeral plan.*

"Work," she said.

"Me?"

"You didn't expect me for free, did you? The world is a market. Be revealed. There is a stall waiting for you at Queen's Crescent Market. Be hire."

Jack went down the stairs, swinging from straight arms, legs crossed. A white newel post was freshly painted. Light slashed through a dusty transom. He went out the door.

"O, the light!"

He shielded his eyes.

"A blinding reality . . ."

Brilliance dripped from the white slab balconies. Iron spikes at the wooded playground gleamed where trees hung still. Jack came to a flat bridge over electrified rails in a ravine. Its walls were chalked blue and white with a Guinness pelican, its pouch full of black Guinness bottles.

Jack threw up twice. A man passing gave him a paper towel.

"Cheers, mate."

A woman passing gave him a breath mint.

"Ta, luv."

There was a red Catholic school and a black playground. Schoolgirls in blazers crossed the road, which went past a buttressed church, cloister and alms houses. The main road, Malden Road, curved. An upside down bird's-eye view of London hung in the window of *Leverton & Sons, Funeral Directors. Sharp's Tackle* sold fishing licenses to the Hampstead Heath ponds. Used furniture crowded the sidewalk. Bicycles shimmered.

"Where's the damn market?"

He stood under a green arch.

"Hey!"

The Queens Crescent market inspector came forward.

"You're late."

"I've been here before, have I?" Jack said.

"Wake up, Jack!"

It was Thursday. The market was on. People crowded stalls with pink and white, or blue and white, canopies.

The sun hit red, blue and green paper birds on sticks, pinwheels, Palmolive soaps, country bread, shoe polish, Colgate toothpaste in red tubes, whisks, rolled black plastic bags, green buckets, red buckets, blue buckets, sour gum drops and Mars bars.

"Hurry up, Jack!"

Jack double-stepped to keep up. Lemons, oranges, and apples — cox, pippins, granny smiths, red delicious and Braeburns — lay in shallow boxes lined with artificial grass. Men shouted from green wood carts.

"Lemons!"

"Cox!"

"Pippins!"

Rhubarb with scarlet and purple stems, turnips, kale, okra, carrots, Brussels sprouts, runner beans lay on green carts and also new potatoes, baking potatoes, Irish potatoes, and little dirt-encrusted button mushrooms.

"Smell the fruit!"

"The dirt!"

A fruiterer with fingerless gloves snatched a striped bag from a nail, slid satsumas into it from a balance scale, twirled it tight, gave it to a woman in a grey coat. She paid him with three coins.

"Thanks, darling!"

He held up more satsumas.

"Satsumas! Satsumas!"

"Are they sweet?" the market inspector said.

"They're all right."

People jostled.

"Your pitch is waiting, Jack!"

"Can I have tea?"

"No."

Blue gloxinia, pink and white foxglove, yellow roses and baby blue hyacinths stood on the black asphalt.

The *Gossip Stop* café was crowded. The *Dreghorn Castle*, in a wall of shops behind stalls, was boarded. *Boxing at the Forum in Kentish Town.* A cartoon sign swung over a carpet store door: two silhouetted men unrolling a carpet. Boys in military sweaters sold bed linen. Lace curtains, black and red handbags, pink hand-knitted chickens, model fighter airplanes were sold under a canopy fixed to a shop front.

A fishmonger wore an Arsenal wool cap.

"Crab! Crab! Crab!"

"Flounders!"

"Mackerel!"

Pitch 66 was a plank on two sawhorses. There was a pile of contraband Calvin Klein socks.

"Stay inside the pitch lines, Jack."

"Will do."

The inspector left. Jack stood behind the plank of socks, leaned back and cupped a hand to his mouth.

"Calvin Kleins!" he shouted. "Contraband and illegal! Socks, my darlings! Come, buy, my sweethearts!"

Next door, at Coles Butchers, chickens, livers, cut beef, salt beef and smoked salmon lay under glass. Lamb, pork and bacon were frozen in white boxes. *Best Irish bacon ribs. Whole collar of bacon £9.99. Irish salt beef. Irish potatoes, cabbage.* Turkey parts were frosted.

A butcher winked.

"We used to butcher horses in the Kentish Town alleys," he said. "Quite illegal, of course."

Across the lane, behind gold letters: GORDON & RUTH'S, winged fairies leaned over a crucifix. A cheetah watched a ballerina. A ceramic rose drooped. A cupid held a mirror to a bride.

There was a poem.

OUR WEDDING
May we always remember
The magic of the day
How it felt to be certain
That love would guide the way
We stand here together
At the threshold of the door
That leads to new fulfilment
From this day forevermore

A fine rain fell. So fine the market lane did not get wet. Gradually it had a sheen.

Jack cupped his hands to his mouth.

"Pound the pair!"

A man at the next stall raised a pale blue shirt in plastic.

"Arrow shirts!"

An old man in a tweed coat stopped.

"Have you anything by Ralph Lauren?"

"What size?"

"Large."

"What colour?"

"Maroon."

"Come back weekend next."

An old man sold pink robes.

"Do you like pink robes?" Jack called.

"I hate them," the old man said. "I spent two weeks in the Royal Free. Never found what was wrong with me. Gave me a lot of meds, though. I had to wear paper panties. Think how that felt."

"Watch my pitch."

Jack went to the *Blue Star Express*. A huge plastic ice cream cone was on the sidewalk. Inside, red vinyl and chrome chairs and chrome tables were crowded with young mothers with small children. The counter had a signed photograph of Stephen Hendry.

"I'll have a jacket potato," Jack said. "White tea."

"Cheese on the potato?"

"Cream."

"Chives?"

"Cheers."

Jack counted his coins.

"Shilling . . . no . . . six pence . . . six pence . . . no . . . no . . . that's not right . . . five pence . . ."

"Sit down."

Jack sat at a table by a window. People passed in black coats. An orange and white sawhorse marked the end of the market. There was a yellow pub with blinds drawn and hanging purple pansies. It was the *Man of Aran*. A Union Jack drooped at a low estate.

Jack read the *New Camden Journal*. There was a death notice. *Former boxer a flower seller at Queen's Crescent. John Russell 'Boyboy'. Encouraged by priest. Fought at Cal-*

edonian Road Baths. A pretty-boy boxer with deft footwork to baffle. Worked at his father's flower and fruit stall. Jack turned a page. *Patient Arson at hostel. The fireraiser was George Charalambous, 46. "I'm quite pleased I've made quite a good job of this one. I seem to be getting better at it." There was £40,000 damage. He heard voices murmurring for him to set a fire. He was formerly of Malden Road.*

"Well, them are those what are worse off," Jack said. "I can't complain."

The cook set down a white mug.

"Your tea, mate."

"Cheers."

Jack poured sugar from a glass canister with a chrome spout. His jacket potato came. He ate. He read. *Brian. Born on the 28th of April. Suddenly passed away on the 12th of May aged 52. He served us as a caretaker for 29 years. I am sure that Brian will be sadly missed by all of us who knew him. He was understanding and very well liked and a person who would assist anybody who needed help. Our deepest sympathy goes to Linda and family at this sad time.* In calligraphy: *Rest in Peace.*

"Better watch your pitch," a boy said.

"What?"

Outside, two young men in nylon jackets scooped up the Calvin Klein socks from Jack's plank.

"Hey!"

"You'll never catch them, Jack."

Jack ran out.

"Those are *my* socks!"

Jack chased them. One tripped at a barrier into the

estates. They threw the socks at him and ran off.

"Chirrah!"

Jack picked up the socks from a puddle and squeezed water out.

"Sods."

He dumped them in a soggy heap on his plank.

"Fifty pence the pair!"

Across the lane three floors of yellow brick apartments for the elderly had a yellow brick chimney. Rain fell harder. Ashdown and Weedington lanes sparkled into Gospel Oak estates.

Jack nudged the plank over the pitch line. The market inspector took out his notebook.

"I warned you."

The market inspector wrote out a ticket.

"I am very sorry, Jack," he said, "but despite being warned you have pushed your plank past your pitch line. Five points. That means you have accumulated a total of more than twenty-five points. Camden Town Hall will revoke your casual stall license. You are a disgrace."

The market inspector left. Jack kicked the plank off its trestles. Calvin Kleins fell into a deeper puddle.

"I didn't even get an awning!"

Jack stood in the rain. He watched water dripping from a blue sign to the Kentish Town Methodist Evangelical Church.

"Now what?"

He went up the lane. Awnings were coming down. Round iron pole-bases with spikes were stacked. A fruiterer rolled artificial green grass. A man hammered stall pipes apart. Two men walked a blue and white canopy together and folded it. Lads threw tote bags into a white van. Men dropped beer kegs off a lorry onto a yellow foam rubber pad and manhandled them down a trap door into the basement of the *Sir Robert Peel.*

Jack went in.

"How's it going, Jack?" the publican said.

"Dreadful."

He went to the bar.

"What'll it be?"

"Local ale."

"This is London. Try the Guinness."

The publican pulled the Guinness tap. Jack looked around. Red leather benches and red leather couches with deep buttons stood at the walls with varnished planters bearing small palms. Black tables in front had cross bars instead of legs. A rose carpet with faded gold crosses went wall to wall. The ceiling was dull white. It was embossed with old rosettes.

A television flickered.

"Come on, England!"

"Yes!"

Jack drank.

"All *right!*"

An old man flailed around the pub.

"I fall," he said, "but I don't fall *down.*"

He took empty crisps bags from the tables, ran his fingers around inside and licked them. Jack sipped his pint. He drank a second pint. A clock with black Roman numerals ticked. He left.

It was night. Sea gulls glided under the green arch and past the houses of the rest of Queen's Crescent across Malden Road. Jack walked past Leverton's. Sikhs locked their doors. A Number 24 bus went by. Flesh flickered green in green-white fluorescent lights.

Brenda sat on the blue couch.

"Lost your job?" she said.

"Something like that."

"How come?"

"Went over the pitch line."

"Did you argue?"

"No."

"I sure can pick them," Brenda said. "When will you get it through your thick head?"

"What?"

"That you're thick."

There was now an embroidered sampler on the wall.

There are rules of existence.
We do not know what they are.
We must obey them.

Jack sat on a straight-backed chair. Calvin Kleins fell into a deeper puddle.

"Cringe."

He cringed.

"Fawn."

Jack fawned.

"Stand up."

"Why?"

"I can break your ankles by my mental power," she

said.

"I don't believe you."

"*There!*"

"Ow!!"

Jack collapsed.

"HA!"

He tottered backward and collapsed again.

"O!!"

"Walk forward, Jack!"

"I can't!"

Brenda laughed.

"NO! YOU CAN'T! DO YOU WANT TO KNOW WHY? YOUR FEET ARE ON *BACKWARDS*!"

"O, the pain!"

"IT'S NOT THE PAIN!" she shouted. "IT'S THE HUMILIATION! WHOEVER HEARD OF A MAN WITH HIS FEET ON BACKWARDS?"

Brenda leaned over him.

"YOU HAVE A FLAT," she shouted. "BUT YOU WILL NEVER HAVE A HOME!"

"O, mercy . . . trust . . ."

"IN THE HOUSE OF TRUST THERE IS NO MERCY," she said. "IN THE HOUSE OF MERCY, JACK, THERE IS NO TRUST."

Jack slept. It was dawn. Brenda opened the curtain. There was a new billboard. *Family Problems? Jennings Son & Ash Solicitors have a Matrimonial Department that deals regularly with divorce and judicial separation. Free consultation. No appointment necessary. Ask for Naomi Turner in our Matrimonial Department.*

"Let us do the *bon ton*!" Brenda said.

"The what?"

"The Chelsea Flower Show."

"Is it on?"

"Be transformed, Jack!"

Brenda put on a black blouse. The buttons were under stress. She put on green eye make-up and deep red lip-stick. She puckered her lips and kissed a tissue. She turned.

"You're not going?"

"No."

"Why not?"

The *Sun* flapped on the floor.

"Because you left the window open!" he said.

"I did not."

"Did."

"You did."

"You."

"Should we close the window?" Brenda said.

"Yes."

"You do it."

"Forget it."

Nobody moved.

"Then what shall we do?" Brenda said.

Time passed.

"Let's decorate!" she said.

Brenda unrolled turquoise wallpaper with gold floral motifs.

Jack stirred the paste, brushed it on and spread the wall-paper on the walls. Cloudy light came in from the bay.

"Turquoise," she said, "is the colour of taste. Turquoise with purple is the mark of the French."

"French?"

"The *fleur-de-lis*," Brenda said.

"It's paisley, duck"

Brenda hung a beaded turquoise chandelier that raised and lowered on a pulley. She raised one ankle behind the other and studied the effect.

"It's fine," she said. "It'll be fine. Everything is ticky-boo. One errs, if at all, on the side of gorgeousness. This was a day well lived."

"Char?" Jack said.

"Lovely."

Jack sliced cucumbers, buttered bread and sliced sandwiches in quarters. He filled Mr. Salmon's green tea pot with boiling water and stirred tea leaves. He served.

"Ta."

Brenda took her tea, smiled and winced.

"Hot."

She held the tea in both hands. A breeze ruffled the curtains.

"Isn't this lovely?" she said.

"It is."

"It is *de rigeur* here in Hampstead," she said.

"Kentish Town."

"Sorry?"

"The sign on Waxham House across the road says NW5."

"That is across the road, sweetheart. Sorry. Our side is Hampstead. Hampstead all the way."

Jack brought butter biscuits. She dunked them. Brenda leaned back, sucking one.

"Your trouble, Jack," she said, "is that you are a Kentish Town person in a Hampstead situation."

Sun came in.

"How I miss the East End," she said. "We had working class markets but they were much grander. Bird shows. Watch fairs! Flowers! Baby fairs! O, the soup kitchens! Jews! We had it all."

Birds twirled in the window.

"One bathes."

She lumbered to the bathroom, undressed and lay in light-crinkled water. She swayed her breasts and slicked her wet black hair. She closed her eyes. Jack came in.

"Shall I get you a towel, luv?"

"Thanks, Jack."

"The orange one?"

"And the pink peignoir."

She got up. Her heavy thigh dripping over the tub's edge. Jack turned away. She towelled and put on the peignoir.

"One is refreshed," she said.

She looked into the medicine cabinet mirror: small, round, freckled face and small black eyes. Dripping hair wrapped in the orange towel.

"O, Christ," she said. "Who made me so unspeakably ugly!"

It was twilight.

"Do we have wine?" she said.

"Yes."

Jack filled a glass.

"The glasses are quite small," she said. "Bring the litre, will you?"

Jack brought the litre.

"I wouldn't drink so much if I were you, Brenda."

"You're not me."

She drank.

"Not," she said, "in the present circumstances."

A blind came down at Dunboyne estate. Droplets, green-blue and red-orange, flared down the window. A sign creaked. Brenda drank. She finished the litre.

"There is an Unwins on the corner, Jack. Will you be so kind as to refresh me?"

Jack went out and came back with another litre of white wine.

"Is it night?" Brenda said.

"Yes."

"I thought it might be."

Jack waved a hand in front of Brenda's eyes. She did not react.

"Shall I not turn a light on, Brenda?"

"No."

"Why not?"

"To be in the dark is fashionable."

She burped.

"Where are you, Jack?"

"Here."

"You are nowhere," Brenda said.

They had mushy peas. Headlight beams caught them.

"O, my God!" Brenda said. "He's pushing peas with his

thumb!"

"Don't like it?"

"No!"

"Then chuck them out," Jack said.

Brenda threw his plate out the window. Somebody yelled and rang a bicycle bell.

"O, right." Jack said. "You're mad. You're bonkers. A right doololly."

Brenda pointed at him.

"I curse you."

She felt her way around the flat.

"Sit down, Brenda."

"Or what?"

"You'll break something."

There was a crash.

"Just an ash tray," she said.

Jack caught her by the wrist She threw him off. She lumbered away. He followed her, groping.

"I hate you!" Brenda said.

"I hate you!"

Brenda turned on a lamp. Jack had raised a knee and bent over, rubbing his hands.

"I am a fly," he said.

"AH!"

"BUZZ!"

He chased her.

"Good Lord, I married an insect!"

"Sting! Sting!"

"HELP!"

A blue feathered tail grew from his backside.

"O GOD, JACK! YOU'RE AN OSTRICH!"

Brenda screamed.

"OUR HATE HAS MADE US CARICATURES!"

They fell asleep sobbing.

"O."

"O."

It was dawn. A billboard was being taken down. Jack threw her nightgown, slippers, panties, and brassiere into the Unwins bag.

"Come on, duck," he said. "A new life awaits."

"O, are we going someplace fancy?"

"The 24 bus."

The Temperance Hospital was on the east side of Hampstead Lane, above Marylebone. It had a charred classical lintel with small, thick-glassed windows that ran along the tops of stained fluted columns. White stones lay at the bases. A black fire escape zig-zagged in a recess in a brown brick wall behind a courtyard. Busts of physicians stood on pedestals.

"The classical," Brenda said.

"Yes?"

"Is best viewed when debased."

Jack carried the Unwins bag through the courtyard. Brenda stopped to breathe. She smiled. A nurse took them to a small room with pale magnolia walls. A bed had a magnolia coverlet with white knotted tassels. There was a pot of water on a radiator. A window looked out on the physicians and a wet purple Japanese maple ruffled. Beyond, through the columns, Hampstead Lane was bright and wet. Two policemen on horses rode toward a stone barracks.

"It's clean," Brenda said.

"Hm?"

"The room."

Brenda patted the coverlet. Jack pulled a package of digestives out of the Unwins bag.

"O, you blessed man!"

"Don't get crumbs."

"They clean."

She ate digestives, a little finger raised. Schoolgirls in green pullovers and grey skirts went by through the columns. Brenda rummaged in the bag.

"You didn't get me — ?"

"No."

"You're no fun."

There was a knock. A nurse brought a blue paper nightgown.

"Hello, Brenda. Is this your husband?" she said.

"Yes."

"Common-law?"

"Common."

Brenda put on the nightgown. Jack turned away.

"Jack. Strings."

He tied the strings in back.

"Nurse," Jack said. "She'll be all right?"

"O, yes."

"She won't go crazy?"

"We have group support."

"Anything else?"

"If necessary."

Brenda clapped her hands.

"O," she said. "I would love a tranquilizer!"

"We hope you won't need one, Brenda. Do you see how calm it is here? You can be calm here, too."

Brenda lay back.

"What happens now?" Jack said.

"Our programme starts at 3:30. There will be an interview with the psychiatrist," the nurse said.

"This is on the National Health, isn't it?" Jack said.

"Of course."

The nurse left. Brenda turned to the door, crossed her eyes and stuck out her tongue.

"*Bbbbrrrrrppp!!*"

Jack went back to the window. Trees with crooked branches, some circling back on themselves, swayed, throwing drops. Cars went by.

"The schoolgirls are gone," Brenda said.

"I was counting the cars."

"Jack."

"Hm?"

"Look at me."

Brenda played peekaboo between her fingers.

"Stop that," he said.

"See? No fun."

Jack sat on the bed.

"I never knew bleakness until I met you, Jack. Don't pretend our problems are all my fault."

She flicked a tear from her eye.

"Can I have a fiver?" he said.

"In my purse."

Brenda nestled into the pillow.

"O, it's much too real."

He kissed her.

"I'll let you get some rest, shall I?" he said.

He left.

"You don't love me," Brenda said.

Jack went to Camden Town. People lined up under The Plaza nightclub's purple awning. Down the high street, rows of three-storey buildings, shops below, had blank windows. In the first block there was no glass. They were black. Crowds moved. Traffic was heavy. A pearly bank of clouds came over north London. Roads diverged to Hampstead, Kentish Town, Holloway and Archway. Jack went down to an underground lavatory, black filigree ironwork on top, urinated, washed his hands and came up. He passed the Inverness Street fruit market and a short humped brick-walled bridge over the Regents Canal. Styrofoam cups bobbed in brown-green water of a white wood lock below a brewery.

A ramp went down past black leather jackets hanging by sand candles, Mexican sandals, belts, stained glass and wrap-around sunglasses. A man in an orange shirt sat on a folding chair under an orange canopy. Behind, the canal was broad, silver and speckled.

"How's my lad?"

"Could be worse," Jack said.

"Lost your job?"

"It was the bloody inspector. Needed a quota. Have you got a watch or something?"

"I do."

"Silver?"

"Plated."

"Okay," Jack said. "I can flog it."

The man handed Jack a watch.

"Sorry that's all, Jack."

"Not to worry. Never to worry. Cheers."

Young people streamed across the road to more market stalls in a stone stable. The windows were barred. Electric bulbs on black cords criss-crossed the stone walls.

Malden Road led past a circular white structure with no windows to the red and gold *Fiddler's Elbow*. A yellow-brick estate with white pillars opened to a concrete courtyard and, behind, a stone church. Lights burned in dark stairwells of the long brown-brick Southfleet estate which ended in a pharmacy across from the *Sir Robert Peel*. It was twighlight. Jack went home.

He sat on a straight-backed chair. Gospel Oak lights came on. He dipped Jacob's high-baked biscuits into a cup of taramousalata.

"We are not happy."

He raised a fist.

"We *want* to be happy."

He danced a jig.

"We *are* happy!"

"HOLA!!"

Brenda was at the doorway, both arms in the air. One hand held the heavy Unwins bag.

"Released!!"

"Already?" Jack said.

"I was persuasive."

She tipped the bag onto the table. A vodka bottle and litre carton of white wine bumped out with a Mars bar.

"What's the Mars bar for?" Jack said.

"Nutrition."

She drank.

"Is it dinner time?"

"I will make you tuna mayonnaise," Jack said.

"With sweet corn?"

"Yes!"

"O, sweet man!"

Jack went into the kitchen. He made tuna fish salad.

"Is it twilight?" she called.

"I believe so."

He picked up two serviettes and the bowl.

"Where shall I put it?"

"On the floor."

"Floor?"

"Right here."

He went into the living room. Brenda sat cross-legged on the floor. Her eyes were closed. The vodka bottle lay at her side, open. She smiled and patted the floor. Jack put the bowl by her knee.

"For you, luv."

Her face fell into the tuna mayonnaise.

"O."

Brenda slept. She woke. It was dawn. Jack drew the curtains. There was a new billboard. *France & Son. Independent Family Funeral Directors. 24 hour personal service. Our Directors will attend at your home to discuss funeral arrangements if required. Chapels of Rest. 7 day visiting. Specialists in overseas transportation. Member, Golden Charter. Prepaid funeral plans. Memorials, stationery. Also at Caledonian Road.*

"Work," Brenda said.

"No."

"I said."

"Where?"

"Teksi mini-cab are hiring."

Jack got a job slipping Teksi mini-cab cards, yellow-and-black, *Teksi 0207 794-2222*, into the brass mail slots of Hampstead homes. He came to a tall, narrow, red-brick Victorian house with steep gables. A black and white tiled walk was lined with blue hyacinths.

A Hampstead artist wearing a wide-brimmed hat and spectacles with a beaded chain bent motionless over a wood crate.

"Ah. There you are," he said.

"Me?"

"My hands are arthritic, you see, and though I am a master print-maker I can not lift this crate."

"I will help you," Jack said.

"I knew you would."

Jack carried the crate up a winding stairwell with a white banister and a grey-green runner carpet under a skylight. An etching of a white Romney Marshes church hung at a landing. The artist opened a door. A living room opened to a bay window. There was a fringed salmon and rust-red rug on a Prussian blue carpet and a grey-green couch at the window where curtains, blue irises and pink tendrils, hung at the sides. The ceiling had a detailed embossed rosette. A bookcase was filled with Penguin editions.

A garden below had a low wood and stone wall covered in vines and ivy under massive Heath trees. A fresh breeze moved segments of the trees in different directions. Leaves showed silver as they fluttered. To the left, a swan ruffled its wings by willows on a cobalt pond.

"A fine garden, sir," Jack said.

"Yes," the artist said. "My daughter is the gardener. A bit dry this summer. Camden Borough has restricted watering. Nevertheless, the climbing roses have done well."

Jack carried the crate down an iron spiral stairwell to a studio. A chalk cutter lay on a scarred table next to a black Remington typewriter. Small wood boxes of scrapers, burnishers, rollers and etching needles with wood handles lay on a shelf over a basin. Bottles of varnishes, inks, turpentines and acids were on a low shelf over the spigot. A pulley with white cord held drying prints. *River Bed, Llandovery.* A lark struggled in tangled roots of driftwood. *Homage to Ralph Vaughan Williams.* There was a red iron press with a brass wheel.

"Shall I put the crate down here, sir?" Jack said.

"Yes."

A girl came into the doorway. She was short-waisted and wore a loose white blouse with wood buttons and embroidery at the cuffs. She had gold-red hair, cut short. Her tan trousers were rolled just below the knees. She wore sandals. Her eyes were green. She wore gold stud earrings.

"Are you going to teach next term?" she said.

"Yes."

"You said we would go to Tuscany."

"I may well teach."

"Will Ludmilla take your class again?"

"I presume so."

"I thought she was going to Warsaw."

"Next spring."

"Are you sure?"

"She might go back," the Hampstead artist said. "She has family in Warsaw. She can do well there."

The girl pressed a finger on the door jamb.

"Do you draw her?"

"Yes."

"Is she naked?"

"When I draw her."

"Are you?"

"No."

"Otherwise you both are decent?"

"Yes."

"She should go back to Warsaw."

The girl left. The artist put a five pound note into Jack's shirt pocket.

"No."

"Please. Absolutely. But I must get to work."

The artist and Jack went upstairs. A door opened. The girl, wrapped in a white towel, hair in another white towel, skipped to her room on the street side of the house and closed the door. The bathroom door stayed open. The floor had white tiles with blue at their cor ners. A deep tub had white lions' paws. Her sandals lay on a round stool. The basin had a wood-framed mirror. A fragrance of soap and warm water drifted out.

"A very fine garden, sir," Jack said.

Outside, puffy white clouds moved in a blue sky past a pale needle steeple on a wooded crest.

"Yes," the artist said.

"The clouds run quick."

She came out of her room, brushing her hair. She wore a pale green blouse but the same tan trousers. She was barefoot.

"Shall I get the post?" she said.

"Please."

She went downstairs. The artist turned to Jack.

"Well, thank you. Goodbye."

Jack went down the stairs. The girl was at the bottom of the stairwell, looking at a Hampstead Fun Fair flyer and an appeal from the Liberal Party. She looked up.

"Are you a criminal?" she said.

"No."

"You have the air."

A toy theatre stood on a table.

"What is that?" Jack said.

"A goblin theatre."

"A goblin theatre?"

"You've not seen one?"

"No."

She turned its key. Caricatures of Hampstead moved: butcher, greengrocer, a coy shepherdess lifted her petticoats to show her ankles, signs on *Perrin's Way*, *Baker's*

Passage, Flask Walk. Children in red oil slicks and red boots carried geese in red satchels.

"Look!" she said. "Christ Church steeple! A squire makes his rounds! Look! The spas are open! With dancers! O, a horrid storm has come but now it is gone and the people are happy! Did you not understand? Children sing!"

"Will you be at the Fun Fair?"

"Yes, of course."

Jack went out. A white van, *Grimsby Fish*, opened. Mr. Grimsby, in a white coat and white cap, rustled in the ice for cod and haddock. At a low ivied stone wall where wisteria had twined into an oak and the oak roots had cracked the stone wall, Jack turned and looked up. The girl sat high in her room at a Queen Anne writing desk with water colour brushes in a jar. An Indian print of a blue crocodile, tail over its back into its mouth, hung by a green curtain. She flexed her right hand and blew on her fingers.

Jack went down a narrow passage between two brick walls. An allée of knobby trees led between ponds. A swan came from under a fallen ivied willow that rested on a cut in a low garden wall. Its wings stirred dark ovals.

Jack burst into tears.

"O, the beauty!"

He covered his face.

"O!"

Boys ran.

"A frog!"

"A frog!"

"Jamie's found a frog!"

A pale path led along a shore of algae to a wooded ravine. Wet steps, orange where split, led to a broken tree that leaned on its own branches in tangled brush. It was getting dark. Birds clacked. Cocoons twirled slowly on silky threads. Two one-branched trees embraced. A black gate led to a thick woods and a narrow path that wound down past a shelter along a sharp-poled fence. Inside the fence, pink leaves covered roots of wet stumps. White filaments grew from black boles.

A stone bridge with brick balustrades crossed a wet oval of black mud. Woody raspberry vines tangled in ferns. Silver-edged clouds moved over rubbing, creaking branches. There was a stand pipe. Agitated white ripples spread. Light hit a bright sham bridge that crossed the corner of a large pond.

"O."

A wet pebble rolled on a bog.

"O."

Birds screeched. A villa glowed.

"O."

It was on a steep lawn embankment, cream-coloured with a pergola of grape vines at an orangerie. The silver clouds sailed in the black glass. Inside, there was a black piano and an oil portrait of a boy in blue.

Jack floundered into the bog. Light dragged through the Heath.

Love will come

He knelt by a hand-cut stream.

"All I ask . . ."

His head lowered —

". . . is to see her . . ."

— to his hand.

". . . one more time . . ."

Light hit his face.

"HEY!"

A guard ran down from the villa. He aimed a torch.

"The light!" Jack said.

Jack shielded his eyes.

"GET USED TO IT!"

Jack ran over the old stone bridge, along the sharp-pole fence, past ferns, pink leaves and stumps. There were love cries.

"O!"

A naked woman humped a mound of ivy.

"O!"

Fun Fair posters sprouted in a grove at the far end of the pale winding path.

"BRENDA!"

Jack ran past *The Freemason Arms* and its huge beer garden, turned at a church, ran past *Curry Paradise*. Black carriage lanterns glowed. He went over a railroad ravine to Fleet Road that curved and became Mansfield Road.

Brenda sat naked on the blue couch.

"Ah!"

"What?" Jack said.

"Flies!"

She swiped flies with a towel.

"O, sin," she said. ". . . sin everywhere . . ."

"Brenda — "

"O, how grotesque you have become," she said.

"What?"

"Where were you?"

"Bloody hell."

She climbed over the back of the blue couch and pointed at him.

"I poison you," she said.

"Drop dead."

She kicked her legs and, arms out, fell to the floor. She shuddered.

"It's the death crisis!"

She clutched her chest.

"Stop joking, Brenda."

"HOW DO YOU KNOW? WHAT DO YOU KNOW? ARE YOU A DOCTOR? OW! OW! OW!"

"Don't scare me, Brenda."

"GOD DON'T MAKE ME SUFFER LIKE THIS!!"

"Shall I call for help?" Jack said,

"DO *SOMETHING*!"

Jack opened the window and leaned out.

"HELP! HELP!"

Somebody banged on the lobby door.

"AMBULANCE!"

"Please come in!" Jack said.

"THE DOOR IS LOCKED!!"

"And you have no key?" Jack said.

"OPEN THE DOOR!"

Jack opened the lobby door. Two ambulance men pushed him aside and carried a gurney up the stairs. One aimed a light into Brenda's eyes. Jack spun around. He slapped his palm three times with the back of his wrist.

"POOR BRENDA!"

"SHUT UP!"

He slumped.

"We've lost her."

The ambulance men hoisted Brenda onto the gurney, covered her with a thin pink blanket and strapped her in. They wrestled her down the stairs into the ambulance. Jack climbed in. He patted her hand. She drew it away. The ambulance curved up Fleet Road to Pond Street and went up past a flower stall and the Royal Free gynaecology annex. It turned into the ACCIDENT AND EMERGENCY. Double glass doors stood behind pylons under a concrete roof with fluorescent lights and, at the centre of the ceiling, a black hole.

Brenda was rolled through the sliding glass doors. A security guard watched monitors by black bottles of carbolic acid. The ambulance men pulled her off the gurney onto a bed. Her eyes bulged. She clutched the pink blanket. A male nurse at the next bed pushed shockers to a man's bare chest. The back arched, rigid. Orange and yellow curtains were drawn around Brenda. The male nurse inserted a needle into her wrist.

"Bring me streptokinase!" he said.

"How much?"

"Five million."

"OW OW OW!"

She stretched her arms to the ceiling.

". . . I commend myself . . ."

Her lips moved.

". . . help . . . help me . . ."

"Brenda — "

"IT HURTS! IT HURTS!"

"Can you not give her a painkiller?" Jack said.

"It's coming."

"WHAT'S TAKING SO LONG?" Brenda shouted.

The male nurse put streptokinase in Brenda's fluid bag.

"Take her out," he said.

Brenda waited in the corridor on a sunken leather chair with tiny black rubber wheels. An old man sat in a chair-scale. There was a black hamper. *Danger Destroy by Incineration.* A young man's head was wrapped in orange bandages. He wore pale green paper slippers. A porter came.

"Are you Brenda Leigh?"

"I am."

The porter wheeled her down a corridor. BONE MARROW TRANSPLANTS. A bank of back-lighted X-rays lined a wall. *Pituitary Tumours and Their Management* by Dr. Bouloux. Etchings of Provence amd Parliament Hill hung in steel frames. SPECIAL INVESTIGATIONS. A lift went up.

"Out."

The Lyndhurst Rooms had a deep blue carpet and a blonde wood counter staffed by women in blue blazers and red scarves. VISA AND MASTERCARD. Arabs waited on chairs with blue-grey plush seats. There was an aroma of rich coffee.

"Not for you, darling," the porter said. "That's private. You're going to National Health."

Stained linoleum led to the Jenner wards. Black scarred oxygen canisters stood by a red vending machine. A trolley with a heart shocker was covered by plastic. *Do Not Remove Equipment from the Emergency Trolley.* Intensive Care was a small room in a corner near the nurses' station. *Don't Send Knives to Anyone in Intensive Care.* The porter wheeled Brenda in. He and a nurse rolled her onto a bed.

"OW!"

The nurse ripped adhesive covers off electrode pads and stuck them on her bare chest and ankles. She fitted an oxygen mask over Brenda's mouth and nose, and hooked Brenda to a monitor. Brenda's oxygen mask fell. The porter picked it up, wiped it on his trousers and put it back onto her mouth.

Jack stepped in.

"Brenda?"

Brenda lay in a mound of pink blanket, tufted black hair, smeared green eyeshade, a black hole under green plastic for a mouth.

"Brenda?"

Don't you know your own wife?

Jack glided to the bed.

"DON'T TOUCH ME!"

The porter took Jack out to the red vending machine.

"Mother?"

"Wife."

"Sorry. Crisps?"

"No."

Jack sat in the porter's chair.

"Don't sit in the porter's chair."

Jack got up.

"Sorry."

A galley kitchen had a pile of small capped urine bottles in wire baskets. Wheelchairs were folded. A physiotherapist carried a dead lamp. A man carried a ladder, bucket and beige rag. A young African woman in a brown checked uniform pushed a tea cart. In the adjacent ward a man fought with his pillow. A priest went by. He smiled. A nurse went down the corridor closing the doors and drawing blinds over the ward's door windows. Two porters followed wheeling a gurney with a long metal box.

"Was that Brenda?" Jack said.

"No."

"Is there a morgue?" Jack said.

"Downstairs."

"Is it cold?"

"Yes."

A nurse came.

"Could you please wait in the Relatives Room?"

The Relatives Room had wood chairs with rose seats on a blue carpet. A video of open heart surgery played silently. There was a yellow folder. ANGIOPLASTY PROCEDURES. The nurse came in.

"Brenda is —"

"O NO!!"

"— in Bay 6."

Jack followed the nurse to the first Jenner ward. Old women, one bald, lay in six beds. A cabinet basin with tall spigots was at the centre of a plate glass window. A brownish haze yellowed the lights on dark Haverstock Hill. Below, a boarded purple-brick church with a low bent purple-brick wall that bulged and had broken from tree roots coming through black earth. A brown door in the ward opened to the toilet. PLEASE KEEP DOOR OPEN WHEN NOT IN USE. A ventilator hummed. A clock jerked but the hands did not move.

"Hi, handsome."

Brenda waved from Bay 6. She still wore the oxygen mask. A green dot spiked on a black monitor. Somebody else's flowers were in a jar on the floor. She sweated. Jack sat in a red leather chair with lion's paw legs and arm rests.

Can you breathe?" he said.

"I can. "

"Good."

"I rather thought it a good idea myself," she said.

Brenda lifted the oxygen mask and sprayed from a white cylinder under her tongue.

"What's that?"

"Nitro," she said.

"How long will you be here?" Jack said.

"Day or two."

"That all?"

"If that."

Lights went off. A nurse went round the dark ward shining a flashlight over the sleepers. She turned to Jack and Brenda and put a finger to her lips. Brenda leaned toward Jack.

"When they put the snake poison in me," she whispered, "I saw that I was sliding fast down a roller-coaster toward either a black obelisk or the same shape was a black doorway. Would I be blocked or go through? I heard: *Either I live or die. Either way it will be an interesting experience.*"

She lay back.

"Death is a lethal thing, Jack. A winged quick thing. Sweet panic. What's wrong?"

"Nothing."

"Your wife dies and you're not listening?"

"I've got something to do."

"At this hour?"

"I need counseling," Jack said. "Shock and all."

"But I'm here!"

Jack reached over her head.

"Look," he said. "A radio. I will turn it on. It will help you sleep."

Her eyes glistened.

"Do you love me, Jack?"

"It goes without saying."

Jack rode the lift. He came out between a library and a Lloyds bank machine. A wall of glassed shops ran along a cafeteria. Teddy bears pressed against the glass. Royal Free mugs were for sale. An old man in pyjamas, hooked to a drip bag on a movable pole, stared at a cup of tea.

Jack ran down spiral steps to Pond Street. *The Roebuck* was brilliant. Old men and old women stretched in the bright Armory. Fleet Road curved past The Beacon. Jack ran around the corner of Waxham House, into the Gospel Oak estates. Glossy black leaves glittered on raised black earth. There was a lighted stairwell. NO HAWKERS. NO CANVASSERS. LONDON BOROUGH OF CAMDEN. A mounded, rough lawn with heavy forked trees ran clear to Southampton Road. Ludham House, on higher ground, was long, white and tiered.

Jack ran onto a green. A black iron ring circled huge trees. Black asphalt was lined with razor wire on a brick wall over the railroad cut. An empty cage was locked. A slab was embedded in the grass. An electric fast train roared, unseen, in the walled ravine. Jack went over a flat bridge. Pink clouds shredded over white Bacton Tower, its elevator lights luminescent, its spiral stairs chained. Jack came out at the *Westport Inn* on Malden Road. NO CHILDREN ALLOWED.

"... the urgency ..."

He ran. Malden Road went straight to the boarded *New Ferry Arms*. A gold *E* was on a black door. A street light leaned against its pediment. Across the road, in the *Fiddler's Elbow*, men sat in pools of light by red pillars with gold capitals. Jack ran across Prince of Wales Road to Clarence Way, a cobbled lane that led to a viaduct.

A Methodist chapel lighted up.

"O!"

The Methodist chapel was black brick with low, stubby black-brick buttresses. Black high-tension wires ran along the roof's broken spine. Half the roof came down to a hedge. A boot scraper stood by a red door with black slits. Jack peered through a slit. Light from Clarence Way came through leaded panes and crawled over an old hardwood floor. Black hooks hung along the rafters. Scissors scuttled. Jack tip-toed in. A page turned in the *Book of Sins.*

Stop, sinner, stop!

Jack stopped.

"O."

Nothing moved. He went slowly down a hall. There was a counting room. Pouches and coin-holders lay on the floor. A green balance scale was on a cabinet. *An Honest Man Is a Gift of God.* Jack went further. A cast-iron coffin with a delicate chain stood upright at an open black doorway to a crypt. DAMAGED BY ENEMY ACTION. Past the coffin a dark room had a communion rail. Pink carnations, purple-tipped, were in a vase by a hymn board. *Anthem 132. Hymn 49, 753, 669, 35. Solo 842.*

Men moaned.

"O."

Methodists cried in the dark. They sat on pews that faced backward. They put the backs of their wrists to their foreheads. *In the resurrection morning I shall rise. To be changed, changed and changed again.* A young man looked up, tears streaming. "Thank you Jesus thank you Jesus thank you Jesus." *A man turned away will look up. I will rise and am rising into originality.* Jack crept down the hall. Doors opened. *The hurt is so deep.* A ladder went into a square black hole in the ceiling. *They may not understand me.*

Jack peered into a kitchen. A woman with frizzy dyed blonde hair, in an apron and yellow dress with white cuffs, stirred oatmeal.

She spooned it into a bowl, added milk, sugar and raisins. A kettle boiled. She poured tea. She put the steaming bowl and a mug of tea on a pewter tray, elongated out the door, carried the tray up a curved stairwell that had no visible means of support, knocked at a door on the landing and went in. She came out without the bowl and tea and carried the tray back down to the kitchen.

Jack ran up the stairs, threw open the door, cartwheeled into the room and grabbed onto a coat rack.

"We must — the two of us —" he said, "— have a conversation!"

A Methodist pastor sat by a fire eating oatmeal. He had white hair and a ruddy face. He stirred the oatmeal.

"What is your name?"

"Jack."

"You are a mess of wounds, Jack."

A red and black Indian rug's tassels spread on a black floor. There were etchings. *Pillar of Fire. The Christian Colliers.* A bulletin board was pinned with notes. *Kenny, Chemotherapy, Whose Mother Is in Holloway. We Also Pray for the McGuinness Sisters, Without Parents.* There was a roster. VISITATION OF THE SICK.

"Where is your lamp?" the pastor said.

"What lamp?"

"The one you used to hold."

Behind the pastor leaded glass windows looked over a wet graveyard tangled in ivy. *My Spirit Had Unquiet Wings.* Wet thistles drooped. *To Trouble Man Is Born.* A mound of wet strawberry tendrils nearly covered a body-snatching spike. *That every mouth may be stopped.* A black iron grave-rail was twined with white morning glory. *That all the world be found guilty.* Mortar had fallen. A few bricks were in wet ferns. *Such is the reward of those who love God.* Droplets came onto the pastor's windows.

"There is a double sun in my breast," Jack said.

"Sit."

Jack sat.

"Soot falls in the back of my mind," Jack said.

"Because of someone?"

"Yes."

"How old is she?"

"Quite young."

The pastor turned to Jack.

"Are you married?"

"I am falling into a new relationship," Jack said. "Of course, there is no relationship. I am capable of a great love."

"Are you married, Jack?"

"My wife hates me."

"Jack."

"What, sir?"

"The one who hates you is not of this world."

Jack's legs cramped.

"You are talking about sin, you know."

"I know," Jack said.

"God has given you grace to believe," the pastor said. "Do not abuse it. Do you see God in this person?"

"Yes."

The pastor chuckled.

"The lives of the religious are very interesting," he said. "Jack —"

"Yes, sir."

"You will not get out of this on your own."

"No, sir."

The pastor stoked the fire. Gold-red sparks cascaded. He gently stepped on them by the tassels of the rug. He brought his chair closer and put an arm on Jack's shoulder.

"Do not be restless."

"No, sir."

"Face your suffering."

Jack covered his face.

"FACE IT!"

Jack dropped his hands.

"Could I have a glass of water?" Jack said.

"No."

"Please."

The pastor held out a pitcher of water. Jack reached. The pastor pulled it back.

"Are you willing to change?"

"O, yes!"

"Or are you just faffing around?"

"No!"

"I don't believe you, Jack."

"I will change."

"Say, *I am willing*."

"I am willing!"

"I AM WILLING!"

"*I AM WILLING!*"

"I don't believe you!" the pastor shouted.

"*I AM WILLING!*" Jack shouted.

"Now you may have your glass of water."

Jack drank. The pastor looked to the ceiling and raised his arms.

"*I lifted a burden*," he recited, "*and look, it had been too heavy for me.*"

"Who said that?"

"I did."

The pastor put the empty glass on the desk. Nobody moved. Jack looked at the clock over the fire.

"The clock has stopped," he said.

"It is a sacred pause."

The pastor drew his chair closer. They were knee to knee.

"Pray with me, Jack.

They closed their eyes, lowered their heads, foreheads on the backs of their wrists.

Bless those who did not get what they came for
Bless those who were confused
Bless those who were not listened to.

The housekeeper elongated into the study with a tray of chamomile tea and honey-graham digestives. Her head came in first then her elbows and shoulders. She took the empty bowl from the desk.

"Thank you, Eloise."

"Do try the biscuits," she said.

She left. Jack and the pastor ate the biscuits and drank tea. The pastor led Jack to the door and onto the landing. The housekeeper had left her hand on the banister. In it was a note. *Souls Must Be Boiling Mad.* They went downstairs.

"Do not be shocked out of salvation," the pastor said, "when you see what you've done."

Jack stepped out. The pastor closed the red door. A constable rode out of the mist on a chestnut mare. By his side was a white mare with no rider. He lifted his hat and sang.

. . . *Me and my Lord* . . .

Lanes led to lanes. A brewery faded. Water dripped from a silver chain on a workhouse door. Blind Methodists followed a rough green strip in the sidewalks past a home for worn-out ministers. Grafton Road was narrow. It went past a printer's shop under a trestle bridge that grazed its roof. Electric boxes were at a viaduct. *The Double Sun* was bright. Spring Place led to Queens Crescent market lane. *The Dreghorn Castle* was now charred. Barriers to the estates were down. *The Blue Star Express* darkly glittered. In *Coles Butchers* beeves winked. White fish flapped. A spider crawled over the wedding poem in Ruth and Gordon's window.

The spider mouthed:

holy

Jack went from Queens Crescent up steps to the long estates angled in Gospel Oak. A stone church was at the centre, across from a French school for girls. Across the green, behind the iron ring of trees, a Somali cultural centre was steel-shuttered in the back of Waxham House. A red C11 bus stopped on Mansfield Road.

The ochre gate was open.

"Brenda?"

Light pools came down the lobby stairs.

"Brenda?"

Brenda sat on the straight-backed chair. Her wrist was red from the needles and the green plastic hospital bracelet was still on. There was a pink glow on her cheek and her small eyes were bright.

"Mm?"

"You're drunk."

"You have been talking," she said, "about me."

"With who?"

"With whom?"

"With nobody."

"Spreading lies."

"No."

"About me."

"Not about you."

Brenda wobbled upright. She tip-toed backward.

"Didn't mean to *pry*," she said. "Didn't mean to *pry*."

Brenda fell.

"Oops."

She pursed her lips.

"Kisses?"

"No."

"See? Something is not right," she said. "No. That is not you. I am going to do it."

"What?"

"Kill myself."

She lumbered across the floor.

"Hoo! Hoo! *OUT THE WINDOW!!*"

"That's not the window," Jack said.

"*WHAT?*"

"It's the door."

"Then I'll go downstairs."

"You can't go downstairs. You can't stand up."

Brenda tumbled down the stairs on her belly, feet first, looking back, startled. She sprawled at the lobby umbrella stand. She blinked, her ruffed hair at odd angles.

". . . how bright the wilderness . . ." she said.

It was dawn. There were no billboards. Jack put her dress, shoes and green eye make-up and wine gums in a Budgens bag and woke her.

"Get up," he said.

"Wha — ?"

"We're going."

"Where?"

"Miss Kelly's."

"What is Miss Kelly's?"

"They narcotize old alcoholic women. It's on Englands Lane near the Holiday Inn. The poison vapors leave the brain."

"It's come to this?" Brenda said.

"It has."

"How long will I be there?"

"A week."

"A WEEK?"

"It will do you good, darling."

"You're a new man," she said.

"I am."

"The pastor changed you, did he?"

"Yes."

Jack combed her hair.

"Let's dance," he said.

She put on green eye make-up.

"For my new life!" she said.

They walked up a cobble-brick path between the Royal Free and the purple-brick church with turrets. Black carriage lamps stood under arching trees. A remnant of a village green, now yellow grass and thistles, was chained off at a black iron gate. On Haverstock Hill, a Chinese man hosed the sidewalk in front of Weng Wah restaurant. Englands Lane went straight, then curved at *The Washington.* Children played in green water behind the plate glass window of a Holiday Inn. Worn steps led to Miss Kelly's.

"Will Miss Kelly's smell of cabbage?" Brenda said.

"Might."

A short white hall led to the reception. Nobody was there. Green foil and gold stars twirled slowly. A green banner with a shamrock hung behind a Christmas tree with red balls. Mock presents lay below.

"Is it Christmas?" Brenda said.

"No."

"Thought not."

Black filing cabinets were topped by faded blue reference books. Two telephone books lay under green-white fluorescent lights. Silver paper hung from a hook.

"No bloody bell," Jack said.

"Let's go home."

"No."

There was a buffet. A basket of rolls on serviettes lay on a chrome shelf by canisters of tea. White coffee mugs were upside down on a towel. Ceramic jam jars were behind a plate of cheeses and ham slices on wax paper. Grey plastic cutlery lay in a gray plastic divider by an eight-slice toaster.

Brenda sniffed.

"Who died?"

Maroon tables stood by a plate glass window looking onto yellow roses in wet gravel. A woman with a fallen bosom, wearing a pleated lavender dress and white beads hanging low, walked past. She had a cigarette holder in one hand and a plate of toast in the other.

"What a vision of loveliness," Brenda said.

A broad-shouldered woman with blue eyes and brown hair in a bun came. She folded her hands in front of her and smiled.

"Hello."

She had a slight Irish lilt.

"I am Miss Kelly. Will you come with me, Brenda?"

Miss Kelly led Brenda and Jack to a white room. A bed

had a blue and pink coverlet. There was a gray carpet and an armoire. The armoire had a mirror in a gold-red frame. A cold draught moved between the bed and a radiator.

"March is a month of rain," Jack said.

"It's not March," Miss Kelly said.

"In England all months are March."

Brenda cried.

"What's wrong, Brenda?" Miss Kelly said.

"I don't want to be here."

"Sure you do."

"It was against my will!"

"She's lying," Jack said.

"*I am so mad I could spit!*"

"Do you want to spit?"

"Could I?"

"Of course."

Miss Kelly brought a sputum mug from the armoire. Brenda gargled with water and spat.

"Visit," Miss Kelly said. "I will come back with a sleeping pill."

Miss Kelly left. As the door closed her long slender fingers were around the door edge. She wore no ring.

"I will never be so happy," Brenda said, "as when I leave this place."

Jack whistled.

"Shall I close the window?" he said.

"No."

"It's cold."

"I like cold."

Brenda sat on the bed.

"Firmer."

"What?"

"The bed," she said. "Than the Temperance Hospital."

Jack fumbled in his coat pocket.

"No smoking," she said.

"Sorry."

Jack put the cigarettes back.

"She seems all right," he said.

"Who?"

"Miss Kelly."

Brenda changed into a nightgown.

"You could sew your own shroud in a place like this," she said. "I want a drink."

"No."

"I SAID!"

"No."

"*Why are you so radiant?*"

"Am I?"

"What did the pastor *do* to you?"

"Nothing."

It rained.

"Can you see the clock in the hall?" she said.

"No."

"Would you go look?"

"Where?"

"Reception."

Jack went into the hall. He came back.

"Two-thirty."

"Thank you."

Brenda ate wine gums.

"I wish it were over," she said.

"It will be."

She rolled to one side.

"Let's kill ourselves."

"No."

"I want a proper East End burial," she said. "Jews and Cockneys. Flowers from Columbia market. A procession down Mile End with eats and drinks."

"Mm."

"YOU! ARE NOT LISTENING! ARE YOU? THAT IS WHAT I AM NOT HEARING!"

"You want to be sectioned, Brenda? Keep shouting."

"*You owe me an apology!*"

"For what?"

"You know damn well! You can not love a fly, Jack. And I am not a fly. Evil is remorseless for queers like you. Only the devil believes he has a right to what he prays for."

An old woman in the next room shrieked.

"*Prays for!*"

Brenda threw the wine gums on the floor.

"I WANT A DRINK!"

"No."

Brenda's eyes bulged.

"HELP!"

Miss Kelly came in.

"What's wrong, Brenda?"

"IT'S HORRIBLE!" Brenda yelled.

Miss Kelly stroked Brenda's hair.

"Well, it's no Fun Fair," Jack said.

Miss Kelly gave Brenda a blue capsule in a white cup. She brought a cup of water. Brenda took it. She giggled.

"My lips are numb."

She sighed. Miss Kelly gently pushed Brenda back onto two doubled pillows at the headboard. Brenda smiled.

". . . so weary . . ."

Brenda snored.

"I'll leave now, shall I?" Jack said.

"Yes."

Jack went out into the corridor.

"You don't think about sex with her, do you?" Brenda said.

Jack went out past *The Washington* through Belsize Park, down wood steps that zig-zagged through a leafy copse to *The Stag* on Fleet Road. The sky was opalescent. Charismatic Christians at the Beacon turned up their loudspeakers.

"O! The double sun!"

> *You are in the grip of a powerful delusion. Do not believe it no matter how beautiful.*

Jack went to the flat and sat on a straight-backed chair at the bay window. Waxham House's green night lights came on. Red garage doors began to glow. The sky was now indigo. Bacton Tower shimmered over Gospel Oak. Pink-bellied clouds came in over the railroad. Down below, on Mansfield Road, a flatbed truck, *Parnham's*, and then anther flatbed truck, *S&D Leisure Simulator Services 0161 835-2785*, took generators to the Heath. A lonely clarinet played from Dunboyne House. The sky was black. Steam came from night lamps.

"How the birds fly," Jack said, "and trees shiver, each with its own secret meaning."

He laughed.

"Good Lord," he said. "I have lived three lifetimes in these past few days."

Jiminy Cricket rolled in on a shorter truck, holding a rolled umbrella. A pink rubber Krazy House of Love went by.

"O, she has exceptionally nice manners," he said. "Such small fingers. What is the worst that can happen? Of course, it would be illegal."

Mansfield Road warped. Jack wiped his face.

"I sweat mercury."

It got foggy. Yellow gourds bounced into the flat and red trumpet vines came through the floorboards. The oven dripped. Dishes broke and the parts re-joined but did not look like dishes any more. Turquoise beads from the chandelier melted and dropped to the floor.

"It's getting dangerous now, isn't it?"

A lizard threw up in a cloud of gnats.

"Christ, I could use a cigarette!"

A maid, black stockings, black skirt, white apron, came through the walls with a tray of Players.

"Thank you."

She left.

"What is that sound I hear?"

He ran to the window. A Jamaican Christian brass band processed down Mansfield Road. The trumpet player turned and looked up at Jack.

"Are you a Christian?"

Jack leaned out.

"Yes!"

"Are you a *Christian*?"

"YES!"

"Are you *willing*?"

"Yes!"

"We don't *believe* you."

"I am willing!" Jack said.

"Are you WILLING?

"I AM WILLING!"

"Then choose."

The Christian brass band circulated back into Gospel Oak.

Jack turned.

"O, the change . . . !"

Jack spun around.

"— magnified —"

He began to glow.

"Glorified!"

He grinned. He tip-toed around the room. He snickered.

"Everything I do is correct."

Jack flickered.

"I CHOOSE THE GIRL!"

His eyes turned silver and his teeth filled with flies. Deformed, he swept around the furniture. Black holes grew in Jack's face. Screaming red polyps came through the floor.

Sing, choir of angels!!

A light went on. Brenda stood at the door. She wore a black leather jacket, black leather mini-skirt and fishnet stockings.

"Ah!!"

"What?" she said.

"Your hair is GOLD-RED!"

"I had it dyed at Shapes, Belsize Park," Brenda said. "Like it?"

"It's bloody startling!"

She turned the light off.

"Brenda?"

"What?"

"Where are you?"

"In front of you."

A heavy tongue flicked. A gray-plated predator walked the room.

"A secret guest lives in our house," it said.

"No."

"Where is she?"

"Not here."

"Then there is a she, isn't there?"

"Yes."

"But Jack, darling. She does not exist. I told you about her at the Chelsea Flower Show."

"We didn't go the Chelsea Flower Show."

"But we did, Jack. Don't you remember? It was so hot. All those white tents. I fell asleep at the Food Court."

"No!"

"Then it was you who fell asleep," Brenda said. "You *do* remember. And I told you about a little girl with gold-red hair."

"When?"

"After the black lilies, Jack."

"WE DIDN'T GO TO THE CHELSEA FLOWER SHOW!!"

"We did, Jack. How would I know about the little girl if I hadn't made her up for you?"

Jack clapped his hands over his ears.

"I DON'T BELIEVE YOU!"

"Yes, you do."

He suddenly pointed at her.

"It was at the Temperance Hospital!" he said. "The school girls passed by the window."

Nobody moved.

"That's right, Jack."

Nobody moved.

"O NO!"

"O, yes."

"But the double sun —" Jack said.

"Sorry??"

"— revolves —"

"Where?"

"In my breast —"

"WHAT?"

". . . to magnify me . . ." Jack said.

"O Jack! You've broken down!"

Brenda came closer.

"Do you want to be sectioned, Jack? Well, I could do

it," she said. "With one little phone call. A man who loves an imaginary girl!"

Jack leaned forward.

"The dull fade, not to grow in grandeur!" Jack said. "I am not a caricature any more! This is about victory or it is about nothing! Even Jesus only lived once!"

"O!"

She backed away.

"How our house has changed," she said.

"It happens."

"The point is, it happens. You should have come to me to verify these things. You cannot verify these things on your own, Jack."

"The world is vile, Brenda! Get used to it!"

"We come to the end," she said. "So now let us kill ourselves."

"No."

"I WILL."

Jack wrestled her into the bathroom, pushed her in and tied the doorknob to the bedroom dresser leg with a long towel.

"I HATED THE CHELSEA FLOWER SHOW!" he said.

She banged on the door.

"We should have had children!" she said.

"O SURE!"

"Why not?"

"God made you homely!"

"O!"

"LOOK IN THE MIRROR!" Jack shouted. "GRAB

IT AND HOLD IT TO YOUR UGLY FACE!"

Brenda kicked at the door.

"You never even proposed!"

"Weren't time."

Jack double-knotted the towel.

"BASTARD!"

Jack put on the black blazer with silver lapels and ran to the Fun Fair grove. Generators throbbed. Hot lights melded high in the Heath trees. A boy pulled a wooden marmot on a red-wheeled wagon.

"It's the Fun Fair!"

Jack wandered into the Fair. A painting of a waitress with a big bosom who served hot fudge sundaes lighted up. White caravans sold pink cotton candy from a counter. A sugar breeze blew. Burgers sizzled. Onions fried. Under the trees a red and yellow carousel turned, mirrors flashing, paintings of the Avon Valley. A red popcorn machine lighted up. Purple steel arms whirled adolescents over the trees.

Loudspeakers boomed.

"BING! BANG! BOOM!"

Jack covered his ears.

"My ears!"

He became green, red and purple. Blue light rotated. Jiminy Cricket turned, thumb up, grinning, holding his rolled umbrella. A man in a red striped coat and top hat passed fire from palm to palm.

"O! The glories!"

Cartoon foxes ate ice cream in a painted explosion. Steam came out of their ears. Jack stumbled.

"Where is she?"

"JUMPING PUMPING KEEP ON THUMPING!"

"PLAY THE GREATEST GAME!"

Toddlers slid down pink tongues between pink rubber pillars. Strobe lights made them stutter.

"*Where is she?*"

"TRY YOUR LUCK!"

"SWEET AND SAUCY!"

"MIND THE AFTERSHOCKS!!"

The Krazy House of Love blew a siren. It had pink bulging rubber walls and crooked black timbers. Painted moths circled a carriage lantern covered with plastic white roses. Painted ivy twined around a real tree. The roof undulated. It had three crooked chimneys and a wood sunflower across its shingles.

"BUY YOUR TICKETS AT THE PIG DESK!"

Jack went out of the Fun Fair grove to a pond by an allée of knobby trees. DEEP WATER. DANGER OF DROWNING.

"Where is the damn girl?"

Two small girls twirled pink plastic umbrellas filled with candy. They wore tiny pink mirrors on their belts. The ponds misted. Lime-green shadows moved. A bird walked on lily pads. A swan moved on dark green water.

"Look! A swan!"

"Do you see it?"

"Yes!"

Jack went to the artist's house. The windows were black. He knocked. A neighbour opened her black window.

"Who are you," she said. "What do you want? Why

are you knocking on the artist's door?"

"Where is she?"

"Who?"

"The girl with the gold-red hair."

"I don't know," the neighbour said. "It is very dark. Have you no light?"

Jank hammered with the lion's paw knocker.

"She is not here," the neighbour said.

"Why not?"

"You know . . ."

"I do not."

"She does not exist."

"SHE EXISTS!"

"Don't shout."

"I met her," Jack said.

"Nevertheless." the neighbour said. "She does not exist."

"We were special friends!" Jack said.

"Were you?"

"She loved me!"

"Did she?"

"WE WERE HAVING AN AFFAIR!"

"At her age?"

The neighbour closed the window. Jack turned around. Leaves flew translucent past black lanterns.

"O, sweet England! Where are you now?"

Jack went back to the Fun Fair. Esmerelda the Swine lay in daisies. Clowns in red and yellow costumes put on pink noses and frizzy orange hair by a stump. Black cables steamed. A red-orange chimpanzee hung from a branch and a clown with straw hair under a pork pie hat looked in the tall grass for his nose. A black donkey in a red conical hat wore a keepsack full of wooden red fish. Jack stole a basket of fruit.

"Brenda!"

He ran home.

"I stole these for you!"

The flat door was open. Jack ran up the stairs. Mr. Salmon and two scaffold lads shouldered and banged at the bathroom door. The towel was on the floor. Blood flowed out around their shoes.

"BRENDA!"

Mr. Salmon kicked the door.

"IT'S NO USE!"

"SHE'S FALLEN AGAINST THE DOOR!"

"BLOOD!!"

Jack threw up.

"BLOOD EVERYWHERE! TOO MUCH BLOOD!!"

Mr. Salmon slapped Jack.

"SHUT UP!"

"IT'S GIVING WAY!"

The door cracked in half. The men pushed the bottom half forward. Brenda slid across the floor. Her face fell over the side of the tub. The men charged in.

"THE BLOOD IS STICKY!!"

"THE BLOOD IS SLIPPERY!!"

"AMBULANCE!"

"THERE IS AN AMBULANCE STRIKE!"

Jack ran down the stairs onto the street.

"HELP! HELP!"

Jack ran through Gospel Oak.

"HELP!"

He ran past the dark Kentish Town Methodist Evangelical Church to bright lights. A crowd roared. Elongated players loped toward the goal. A black trestle bridge had electric girders, barbed wire that dripped.

"HELP!"

O'Reilly's pub was red with gold-red globes and mirrors behind the counter. Jack ran in. The floor was worn hardwood. Couches were at the Holmes Road windows. Irish men sat on stools. They turned. In the long mirror: the backs of their heads and a clown with an arrow through his head.

"WAAAAH!!"

"Easy, mate."

The men came closer.

"EEEYOW!"

"Do you need help?" the publican said. "No? Well, we can't have this sort of thing here."

The publican took Jack by the elbow and collar and threw him out the door. A constable held a light into Jack's eyes.

"THE LIGHT!"

"Calm down."

The constable put the light in his pocket.

"What is your name?"

"Jack."

"A bit banged up, are we, Jack?"

"Did you hit me?"

"No."

The constable turned Jack's face.

"Ow!"

"No syringes?"

"No."

The constable put on white gloves and went into Jack's pockets.

"Nothing."

"I told you."

The constable slapped a hand on Jack's shoulder.

"Jack."

"Don't shout."

"Jack."

"What?"

"This way."

The constable took Jack around the corner onto Holmes Road. *24 Hours Emergency Criminal Services.* A brown-rimmed clock, *Leverton & Sons*, with black Roman numerals stuck out of the corner of a store. Two black light poles had two green-blue lights and a third blue-green light lower down that stared at Jack.

"Is a German polka playing?" Jack said.

"No."

The Holmes Road police station began to glow. It was recessed, a sheer orange-brick wall behind glossy shrubs, with one large black window that reflected a scarlet building with steep gables. A black arch curved over an entry walk. A blue lantern hung from its centre, with white letters: POLICE. The constable took Jack to a glossy black door in a huge round-topped door to the parking lot.

They went up a ramp to the side of the station.

The constable pressed a white button. A glass door unlocked. He opened it.

"In."

Jack went in. The constable pressed a black button. A black door unlocked.

"In."

Jack went in.

"Calm down, Jack."

Most lights were off in the charge room. The floor was old black linoleum. A custody officer looked up from a scarred metal desk. He sat on a torn leather chair. He wore a tie with a maroon bell, book and candle. A low bench ran along a wall.

"Sit."

Jack sat. The custody officer turned to the PC.

"Are you the arresting officer?"

"I am."

"What's his name?"

"Jack."

"What is the nature of the offense?"

"Public nuisance."

"Where?"

"O'Reilly's pub," the constable said.

"When?"

"Five minutes ago."

The custody officer chuckled.

"Didn't have to bring him far. Did you?"

"No, sir."

The custody officer studied Jack.

"Do you work, Jack?"

Jack stood.

"Sit."

Jack sat.

"I was a casual stall holder at Queen's Crescent market."

"Off Malden?"

"I was a dealy man," Jack said. "Calvin Klein socks. That's what they told me."

Jack spat in his hand.

"Done!" he laughed.

The custody officer picked up a pen.

"No fixed abode?"

"No, sir. Not now. Doubt it."

Jack separated his fingers and peered between.

"Peekaboo!"

The custody officer folded his arms.

"This is the Kentish Town police station, Jack," he said. "You are not a clown. This is not a circus."

"O, no, sir," Jack said. "It is not fit to be a clown in the Kentish Town police station. Not in the present circumstances."

"What present circumstance?"

"O me. O my . . ."

"Did you kill someone?"

"How the hell should I know?" Jack said.

The custody officer turned to the constable.

"What do you think?"

"Section 136, sir."

The custody officer turned back to Jack.

"Do you want to be sectioned, Jack?"

"No."

"We could do it."

"Could you?"

"We can take you to the Royal Free. Let a psychiatrist look at you. Then take you to Colney Hatch. Ever been there?"

"I don't want to go to the Royal Free."

"Why not?"

"Too much blood."

"Where does the blood come from, Jack?"

"Me to know and you to find out."

"Be civil."

"You be civil," Jack said.

"Shut the lid."

"Okay. It is shut," Jack said.

"Shut it properly."

A medical officer came in. He wore a maroon coat.

"What's his name?"

"Jack."

"He's trembling."

The medical officer came closer.

"Can you stand, Jack?"

"Not sure."

"Stand, please."

Jack stood. He sat abruptly. He laughed.

"Oops. That didn't work, did it?"

"Try again."

Jack stood.

"Into the medical room. There. By the ladies room."

Jack went into a medical room. It had a high grey bed. A thick translucent window looked over the ramp. The medical officer washed his hands. The constable leaned at the open door, arms folded.

"Take off your shirt."

Jack took off his shirt.

"On the bed, Jack."

"Lie?"

"Sit."

The medical officer swung a lamp into Jack's face.

"Who hit you?"

"I don't know."

He listened to Jack's chest, tapped Jack's knees with a rubber-headed hammer.

"Ow."

"Does it hurt when I press here?"

"No."

The medical officer looked into Jack's throat, ears and eyes. He took Jack's blood pressure.

"Good Lord. Are you on drugs?"

"No."

"Pull down your trousers."

Jack pulled down his trousers.

"Bend over."

The medical officer spread Jack's buttocks.

"Were you brought by the Jig Saw Unit?"

"The what?"

"The Sapphire Unit."

"What's that?"

"The sexual offenders squad."

"No."

"Thought you might have been."

He wiped Jack's bum. The custody officer came in. Jack pulled on his trousers.

"Get him a sandwich."

The constable left. He came back with a chicken salad sandwich.

"God bless," Jack said.

Jack ate.

"I need to piss," he said.

"In the ladies room."

Jack went into one of the cabins in the ladies room. There was no door.

"All through?"

"Yes."

"Would you like to wash your hands?"

"Thank you."

"Your face, too," the custody officer said.

Jack washed his face.

"That's enough."

"Shall I give you the towel now?" Jack said.

"Please."

The custody officer dumped it in a hamper.

"Are we going somewhere?" Jack said.

"Yes."

"Is it far?"

"No."

"Broadmoor?"

"Not that far."

"Will you handcuff me?"

"No."

"Will I be raped?"

"Shouldn't think so."

They walked past the desk to a room cluttered with cardboard boxes. To the left was a short corridor of six scratched steel doors with white handles. The custody officer unlocked one with a key into a white handle.

"Dead bolts."

He opened the door.

"In."

Jack went in. Rain fell at a high white-barred window. The wall below was streaked. On the ceiling, a black printed stencil: *Crimestoppers 0207 435-9898.* A long plank came out of the far wall. It had a folded brown blanket. A fluorescent light was on. A lidless steel toilet was by the cell door next to a call button.

"It is the largest cell we have, Jack."

"Okay."

"Lie down."

Jack sat on the plank. A train went by, slow and heavy.

"Kings Cross?" Jack said.

"St. Pancras."

"Is it still raining?"

"No."

"Feels like it."

"Wrap yourself in the blanket, Jack."

Jack wrapped himself in the blanket.

"Who did you kill, Jack?"

"Nobody."

"You're a sad bastard."

"Everybody is."

"I have to close the door, Jack."

"Okay."

"It is a sound you won't forget."

The door was heavy and the slam ricocheted up and down the corridor. Jack covered his ears.

"JESUS CHRIST!"

The custody officer opened the wicket.

"I told you."

He slammed the wicket shut.

"GOD!!"

The custody officer left. There was a telephone call.

"Yes, we heard about the blood. Where is she now?" the custody officer said. "No point, is there? The coroner's okay with it? Okay. What? I don't care. Get rid of it. Fine."

Jack crawled on his knees and the blanket slipped to the plank. He stood and spread his hands on the wet wall. He rubbed his cheek against the mold.

". . . in the twinkling of an eye . . ."

Outside, there was a sound of something like wet cardboard being struck by something hard. Jack peered out. A man groaned. The cry changed. Two Asians ran away, one with a cricket bat. A white man chased them. A police helicopter came over Kentish Town. The searchlight went over the canal.

"O, horror!"

The custody officer opened the wicket.

"Jack, I am going to bail you to the police station. Do you understand? You must come back in three days."

"Why?"

"You have things to do."

He led Jack into a veneered corridor and then to a reception area with a community bulletin board and two windows. A boy translated for his Saudi mother. Jack stepped out. Lights red, amber, green came through fog. An African woman in high heels clicked by. A smoke-stack rose behind the Holmes Road depot.

He came to Mansfield Road. Blue scaffold joins and yellow ropes were piled below the bay window, *E&D Roofing 0207 485-2222*. The door was open. Jack went in. Brenda's clothes lay in a heap. Cardboard boxes were filled with melted turquoise beads and scraps of turquoise wallpaper. The white door still had the skeleton key with its string. A new balustrade square-cut, was freshly painted. An old man in white denims smoked on the landing.

"I am the decorator," he said.

Mr. Salmon carried the mattress down the stairs.

"O, you found the blazer in the closet. Good lad. Come in! See the flat!"

The flat was now pale blue. A beige couch, extra large, with oversized pillows and a ruffled skirt, stood on a new blonde hardwood floor. Track lighting replaced the chandelier. There was an Ikea music cabinet.

"Nice, isn't it?" Mr. Salmon said. "I call it the Highbury look."

A van went by with a horn-speaker. *Attention, landlords! Fine new properties for the discerning tenant. Available now on a limited basis at Foxton's!*

"What's going on?" Jack said.

"A property boom," Mr. Salmon said. "Everybody is a landlord now."

Jack walked the flat.

"There is a broken tea pot on the floor, Mr. Salmon."

"I know."

"Who broke it?"

"You did," Mr. Salmon said. "Who else would break a tea pot and not pick up the pieces?"

The kitchen floor platform and wood posts with braided rope were gone. The floor was now grey and maroon with white grout. Long-necked chrome taps were on a new stainless steel basin. Green curtains hung at the window.

"Brenda's dead," Mr. Salmon said.

"I know."

"It would have been better to have been human, Jack," Mr. Salmon said. "That was your mistake."

Mr. Salmon ran to the landing.

"Don't forget the Monet!"

He came back.

"Could I use the loo?" Jack said.

"You know where it is."

Jack went through the bedroom. A new box spring mattress lay by an as yet unassembled white dresser on new beige carpet. The bathroom door opened outwardly. Broken tiles lay at the threshold. The tub was smaller but had a glass door instead of shower curtain. A wall was gouged where the medicine cabinet had been. The same window looked onto the brick wall outside.

He read the *Ham & High. Jacinte Eileen Payren. Passed away 26 May. Mr and Mrs McCaffrey would like to thank all family and friends and neighbours for all the floral tributes and messages of sympathy in the death of their daughter Jacinte.*

"Do you want the property section?" Jack shouted.

"No."

Jack turned the page.

Girl heard screaming. Beaten in King's Cross. Lucas House, Argyle Walk was a place of prostitutes and drug dealing. Shouts and screams from a teenage brothel.

"Wash your hands, Jack."

Jack washed his hands. He went back to the living room. Blue lightning flickered over Dunboyne estate.

"Is it Sunday?" Jack said.

"No."

"It always rains on Sunday."

"It's not Sunday."

Scaffold lads climbed to the roof.

"A nasty day," Jack said.

"The work must be done," Mr. Salmon said.

"Does it?"

"It comes to be done. I've a mind to sell this flat," Mr. Salmon said. "Two hundred thousand."

"For this dump?"

"Oh, they'll buy. They'll buy. Why? Are you looking?"

"No."

"Can't get the dosh?"

"No."

A scaffold lad carried a yellow rope and propane tank up the scaffold.

"Can I stay here?" Jack said.

"No."

"I've got no home," Jack said.

"Not to worry," Mr. Salmon said. "Homes are provisional."

"Now?"

"Always."

Mr. Salmon turned.

"Look! An English phenomenon!"

"What?"

"Wall fungus!"

Workmen carried out bits of old blood-flaked black and white bathroom tiles in a dustpan.

"Coffee?"

"Cheers."

Mr. Salmon turned on a kettle in the kitchen.

"Instant?"

"Cheers."

"How do you like it?"

"Weak."

"Coffee weak or milk weak?"

"Milk weak."

Mr. Salmon came out with a paper cup of coffee. Jack used two hands, trembling.

"Oops."

"Spill?"

"Sorry. New floor," Jack said.

"Paper towel."

"Where?"

"Floor."

Jack wiped the spill.

"Baked beans?" Mr. Salmon said.

"Sorry?"

"You can have some baked beans if you want."

"God bless."

"Cold."

"Fine."

"I'd just chuck them out anyway," Mr. Salmon said.

Jack ate out of the can.

"Where is she?" he said.

"Golders Green crematorium."

"Already?"

"It's been days."

"Just one," Jack said.

"Days, Jack. You can't account for them. Everybody else can."

"Who paid?"

"Camden Services."

"Then there is no debt," Jack said.

A car slowed. Jack drank coffee from a saucer.

"I'm skint, Mr. Salmon."

"Weep, you poor bunny."

"Please," Jack said.

"I, too, have suffered."

"Please."

"There's coins in the coffee can."

Jack took the coins. He kicked a window. It shattered.

"Thanks, Jack."

"Pleasure ."

"Okay, cowboy," Mr. Salmon said. "I got work to do."

"It's cold."

"It's my flat."

Jack tossed the coffee on the floor.

"Guess I'll go get Brenda," he said.

Jack went to the Heath ponds. WATERFOWL HAVE BEEN INJURED OR KILLED BY BECOMING ENTANGLED IN FISHING LINES. DO NOT DISCARD LINES OR TACKLE. NATIONAL RIVERS AUTHORITY BAILIFF. The Fun Fair grove was frosted. Birds pecked at pebbles. A clown needle-poled scraps, A black mastiff sniffed the tyres of a caravan with its counter open. A torn red sweater hung on the black coupling ball. A twelve year old girl with a pink beret sold tea.

"What are you calculating?" she said.

A high-pitched bird shrieked.

"O."

Up the winding road by a mansion block an old woman with stiff orange hair spread her coat and puckered her lips.

"Kisses?"

Death Is My Authority

Jack climbed to the crest of the Hampstead Heath massif. He passed *Jack Straw's Castle.* The road divided. North Road wound down between steep black mesh-reinforced earth banks. Trees of the Heath spread overhead into a milky sky. Drops split as they fell. Far away, blue snow clouds rolled over the North Circular. He passed the *Bull and the Bush.* The road straightened to Finchley Road. He took a quiet road past a stone church. Pale packed effaced tombstones leaned back and faced the blank sky. A gap in the church wall was strung with barbed wire.

Across the road, a black gold-flourished gate opened to an asphalt court behind which was a terracotta roofed Italianate cloister with an orange-brick tapered chimney. IT IS INAPPROPRIATE TO LET CHILDREN RUN AND PLAY IN THESE REVERED GROUNDS. *Leverton & Sons* and *Kenyon* hearses were parked. Heat rippled from the chimney.

Jack went through a roofless court. Wood slats were stapled with dormant wisteria. White plaques lined the walls. *Government chemist. A tribute from his colleagues, friends and sons. The Dark Shall Be Dispelled. Our souls shall radiate with light and glory. Father I Fear Not. This tablet is dedicated by the Agents' Association in the revered memory of Archie Parnel.* Two swans faced each other on a black lacquer plaque. A yellow leaf floated in a concrete tub. Outside, on the edge of the grounds, a *Pro Patria* temple with four pillars and a blue ceilinged classical half-dome stood by pruned dormant roses in black earth. Each rose had a black iron card holder on a black iron ring. Pink algae moved around a dribbling standpipe in a concrete tub.

A train left for Edgeware.

"O."

More woody vines and plaques were on a wall. *The Marble Of Living Stone Is By Love Burst Asunder. In Service*

Of A Foreign Mission. The kiss of the sons for paradise. Forget No We Never Will. Happy Days Mum And Dad Re-united. He went down a flagstone cloister walk. Black carriage lanterns hung from a peaked wood roof. A few sarcophagi gleamed on the wet grounds. *Cohens may witness from the corridor.* Red bouquets lined the wall. Petals of a blue and white wreath formed the Hindu holy word.

Jack took the wreath.

"For you, Brenda."

Petals scattered.

"O."

He carried it to the chapel. Empty pews on a black and white marble floor faced red roses in a black hoop at the front. A young man in grey swallowtails and white gloves stood at a catafalque with a casket by a black velvet curtain in a wall. He knocked three times. A black tooth lifted at the rear of the casket and pulled it through the velvet.

"Was that Brenda Leigh?" Jack said.

"No."

"Then I'll keep the wreath."

Jack went into a Memorial Hall. It was cold. A marble floor was incised *Alpha*, *Omega*. Light from a small high window in a concrete wall fell in silver shafts through dust onto an altar covered in white linen. Pews were empty. Pink carnations splayed out from green sconces. There was an open book of names. THE BURNING OF ANY SUBSTANCE IN THE CHAPEL IS STRICTLY FORBIDDEN THIS INCLUDES CANDLES. *Applications for Blue Leather Panel and for Book of Remembrance.* Com-

memorative Vases price list. Jack turned to go. At the inside of the door tiny Santa Clauses, teddy bears and miniature soccer balls hung on pegs. *Who Died in the Month of His Birth. Precious baby asleep in our arms.*

Jack went down to a columbarium.

"Brenda?"

A skylight glowed white over rose petals in a silver bowl and a map of names on a varnished mahogany table. Niches around the room contained miniature caskets, vases and sarcophagi. A cut-glass flower-holder stood between a tiny black slab and onyx casket. A goblet held polished pebbles. Hand-written cards were stuck in tiny copper mail holders. *Gainst Storm & Wind & Tide. For as long as there is memory. Cherished among those who fell asleep. Who was called to higher service.*

Jack huddled in his torn black blazer. The silver lapels dangled. A figure moved furtively down narrow winding stairs.

"Who . . . ?"

The figure was gone.

". . . nobody . . ."

Jack walked out, crying, dropped the wreath and stumbled into an alley between orange-brick walls. There was a hum.

"O?"

He peered in. A dirty skylight full of twigs in a white vaulted ceiling let light onto a steel bank with three wood panels.

"O."

Jack scuttled into a prop room. Crucifixes, a Star of

David and a Krishna leaned against a black vinyl couch by a table with a coffee machine. *The difference between a coffin and a casket is the shoulder width.* Green physicians' slips were spindled on a desk. *Baby coffins are free.*

There were three knocks at the wall.

"O."

A young man in black trousers turned a brass crank. A casket from the chapel rolled in onto his catafalque through a small window. He rolled the catafalque to the steel banks and pumped it up to a panel's height. The hydraulic fluid leaked. He pressed a green button. The panel lifted. Silent flames roiled in from the sides and bottom of a long black chamber. He shoved the casket as hard as he could over the rollers.

"Charge!"

The casket bumped in. It smoked. A brass name plate slid off. The casket ignited. People sang a hymn behind a wall.

"Hymns . . . good . . . drowns the rollers . . ."

Hand over hand, he stilled the clattering rollers. Jack ran down the side of the machines. *Putrefaction is dangerous.* It got warm. *Cancer Patients Take Longer. Fat Sends the Temperature Flying.*

"Brenda?"

A crenellator chugged on a wood counter by brass canisters and a white plastic funnel in a small room. White plastic jugs with black tops lined a shelf. Jack read the name tags.

"Where is she?"

A machine hummed. He turned.

"O."

Three machines had round steel doors with round black peepholes. Jack peered into the first peephole. The black top of a still head lay in silent curling flames. *Abner Frisham.*

"Such serenity . . ."

He peered into the second peephole. *Until No Physical Flame.* Red and gold-brown embers pulsed. *Henry Wainright.*

"How beautiful . . ."

He bent down to the third peephole. The chamber was cool. Grey-white ash and bone bits lay in the dark. *Brenda Leigh.*

"BRENDA!!"

He yanked the door open. Ash settled to the floor.

"O! No!"

He grabbed a long-handled rake by a red oven mitt and raked the ash and bone bits into a steel box below the lip of the door. He funnelled the ashes into a canister.

"Hey!"

The young man in swallowtails dropped a bouquet of red roses by the side of the machines.

"What are you doing?"

"She's to have a proper East End funeral!" Jack said.

"What?"

"Jews! Watch fairs!"

"YOU'RE DRIPPING!"

"*What?*"

"It's got a false bottom! It's for garden burials!"

Jack clutched the canister. The young man chased him

onto the grounds. It was twilight. Sleet fell. They ran past a mausoleum at a wall pocked by old shrapnel. A black-plumed horse stamped at a black-plumed carriage.

Jack tasted ash.

"O!"

Ash settled on the silver lapels.

"O!"

The grounds got spongy. SUFFOLK REGIMENT. ROYAL FIELD ARTILLERY. LONDON IRISH RIFLES. *To have loved so deeply.* A braided urn dripped. *Frequent I Now Fields of Hosannas.*

"Stop!"

Jack jumped off a miniature Japanese bridge, splashed through lily pads and ran past a Serenity Lodge. The grounds narrowed. Pines came forward. There was a green wall.

They wrestled.

"AH!"

"HAH!"

Jack pulled himself up the green wall by one arm.

"AH!"

Love knows not its depth until the hour of separation.

"Ha!"

He kicked the young man in the face.

"O!!"

Jack fell over the top into an allée of pink leaves between the green wall and a brick wall in front of elegant brown houses. Huge branches from both sides reached down to the leaves, up again, intermixed, creaking. Jack was on his hands and knees.

"A sudden, awful silence . . ."

A bird clacked.

"How fearful . . ."

A big dog, unseen, sniffed.

"Where — ?"

Jack turned round.

"Where is the damned sow?"

The canister was spinning through pink leaves, spitting ash.

"BRENDA!!"

He scooped ashes, twigs and pink leaves into the canister and limped to a green iron gate at the end of the allée. It had green gables over green posts with nippled caps. Green teeth pointed from a diagonal green bar and green teeth pointed up from a bottom green bar. A green padlock had rusted. Jack carried Brenda over the gate onto an asphalt path by a low-roofed house wall, past a flickering carriage lamp to concrete posts at a road.

It was night.

"It is the Heath, Brenda. And it is night. But we shall not be afraid for I am with you."

Jack carried her into the Heath. A hazy moon glowed. Silver long grass swirled on a long slope. Root balls of fallen oaks lined a ditch. Mounds steamed. Far away, black filigreed trees humped at the blank windows of Golders Green houses with silhouetted chimneys. Smoke drifted low.

Crows swarmed.

"O."

Water dripped.

"O!"

Jack groped. A funerary basin with a stone lion's head stood alone. A locking gate opened. Jack crossed into a woods, past a stone dairy, through a green iron cage with rotating bars and under a pergola of woody grape vines. It ran along the orangerie of the villa. Below, down a steep grassy embankment, the white sham bridge lighted up on a black pond. The stone bridge lighted up at the bog.

"... the bridge ..."

Jack tripped. He rolled down the embankment. The canister bounced over the hand-cut creek and splashed in the wet black oval. It bumped. It turned upside down, the false bottom flashed, and it sank. A duck pecked bobbing ash.

"Hey!"

A Hampstead Heath constable came around the villa.

"You wretch! What did you throw in the pond?"

White light hit Jack in the eyes.

"Nothing!"

"Liar!"

"I am blind!" Jack said.

"I don't believe it!"

Jack lowered his head, arms forward, and banged into a tree.

"See?" he said. "Would a sighted man do that?"

"Get in the jeep."

The Hampstead Heath constable drove Jack to the Holmes Road police station. The custody officer came out.

"Do you have a place to stay, Jack?"

"No."

"What shall we do with you?"

The Hampstead Heath constable signed a paper and drove off. The custody officer gave the papers to a constable and locked Jack in the back of a police car.

"Am I not to bring a plastic bag for my clothes?" Jack said.

"Do you have other clothes?"

"No."

The constable drove Jack out the Regis Road exit over a railroad cut to Kentish Town Road. A market of green poles and a glass peaked roof was empty.

Jack sobbed.

"It was to have been beautiful!"

"That was your wife, wasn't it?" the constable said.

"Who?"

"The one you threw into the pond."

"Yes."

Jack kicked the iron mesh between the front seat and the rear seat.

"Restrain yourself."

"Or what?"

"Others will."

The old Copenhagen market was now a huge lawn with a memorial tower. The police car turned at Caledonian Road.

HM Pentonville Prison had an enormous black door with carriage lanterns at the door pillars. White-barred windows ran from an oversized pediment. A smokestack rose from the roof. Pollarded trees grew out of a courtyard behind the tall white wall with a black bottom border.

The police car drove to the rear.

"Out."

Jack got out.

"I need rest," he said.

The constable led him to a door.

"In."

Young men sat on soft beige couches. Some stood. The floor was scuffed maroon linoleum. A clock ticked. A caramel stain branched around ceiling holes. A prison officer in a short-sleeved white shirt and black tie sat at a desk in front of a bright mesh-reinforced window.

"Sit."

Jack sat.

"Surprised to be here?"

"Yes."

"You are here for a short time. You don't behave, you'll be here longer."

There was a sign.

> *Under the Prison Act 1957 it is an offense for any person*
>
> *i. to help an inmate escape or attempt to escape; the maximum penalty is 10 years imprisonment (section 39 as amended)*
>
> *ii. without authority to convey into the establishment or to an inmate intoxicating liquor or tobacco; the maximum penalty is 6 months imprisonment or a*

£1000 fine or both (section 46 as amended)
iii. without authority to convey or attempt to convey into or out of the establishment or to an inmate any letter or other article or to place it outside the establishment intending it to come into an inmate's possession; the maximum penalty is £100 fine (section 41 as amended)

The officer at the desk beckoned.
"Come to the desk, Jack."
Jack went to the desk.
"Stand still."
Jack stood still.
"Why are you wearing a black blazer with a silver lapel?"
"It just happened, sir."
Cards with names stood in metal slots. The officer examined Jack. *New external scars. Left side of face, below eye.* He handed Jack a clipboard.
"Tick the boxes, please."
Jack ticked boxes.
"What will you do to me?" Jack said.
"We will take a picture of you and verify who you are and that you know why you are in prison."
"Why am I?"
"Nobody knows what else to do with you."
Jack followed a prison officer to a short low corridor with green walls bathed in a green light. Yellow chairs were stacked by a trolley. There was a brown door. BLUE MOP ONLY.

"No valuables?" the prison officer said.

"No."

"Lice?"

"No."

"Sure?"

"Pretty sure."

"We can destroy your clothes."

"I have no lice."

Another prison officer came.

"How is he?"

"No lice."

"He says or you know?"

"He says."

"Let me see."

The second prison officer bent Jack's head forward and fingered Jack's scalp.

"No lice."

"I told you," Jack said.

Two shaved-headed young men smiled. They wore grey track suits and runners.

"Hey."

"Hey."

They shook Jack's hand.

"Friends."

"This is Jack," the prison officer said.

"He's my lad."

"You'll like it here. We all do."

The boys left. One turned back and curled a fist. He smiled.

"Go Islam!"

"Put your clothes in the basket, Jack," the prison officer said. "The muddy blazer, too."

"All my clothes?"

"Absolutely."

Jack put his clothes in a basket. He shielded his genitals.

"I want you to shower, Jack."

"Where?"

"In the shower room. Once you have showered, you will put on a track suit and runners. I will take you to a room where you can rest. Use the astringent soap."

Jack showered and came out.

"Shower!" Jack laughed. "Hot!"

He toweled and put on track trousers and a grey sweatshirt.

"Are you Welsh?" Jack said.

"Yes."

"Are all the prison officers Welsh?"

"Some are from the North."

"It's expensive in London, isn't it?"

"We get a per diem."

Double white steel doors stood at the end of the corridor. KEEP DOOR LOCKED AT ALL TIMES. The Welsh officer unlocked them.

"In."

Jack went into the space.

"Do the men gratify themselves?" Jack said.

"It is a busy place."

The Welsh officer locked the double doors behind and unlocked the double doors in front.

"Out."

Jack went out. They were on a mezzanine. Below, a long green floor led past a long row of small green doors with black numbers. It was warm. There was a buzz. There were call bells at each door. Further down were white steel stairs with mesh over them.

"YOU WHITE MEN PUT YOUR PANTS ON BACKWARD AND GO BLAH BLAH BLAH!"

"FUCK YOU!"

"SHUT YO' MOUTH!"

"Come down with me, Jack."

"It is so energized!" Jack said.

"Quickly, I say."

They went down. The walls sweated. Globules floated, struck by pale light. Two faces peered from a small slot.

"Hi."

"Hello."

Prisoners mingled with prison officers on the main floor. A prisoner mopped the floor. He looked up.

"Nice to see you," he said.

It got hotter. A black prisoner pushed a trolley with two blue bottles of water. He nodded to Jack.

"How's it going?"

A prisoner bumped Jack. Suddenly the Welsh officer threw him against a wall and wrestled him down. Two more prison officers ran in and knelt on the prisoner's chest and neck. The Welsh officer stood, red face, breathing hard, and stepped over the prisoner's head and punched the air.

"Adrenalin!"

They went to the Centre. It was semi-circular. The floor was black rubber except for a purple border along the curved wall. Four long corridors radiated, each with white steel gates. Prison officers stood at a bolted desk by the flat wall. A white rope hung from a green radiator. A black iron bell sat on a wood cabinet.

"Stay on the purple border, Jack."

"Yes, sir."

The Welsh officer went to the desk.

"LOVE YOU!"

"FUCK YOU!"

"*JOKING!*"

A black prisoner came in from one of the corriors and replaced an orange tag on a blackboard on the purple border. PV 145. HM PRISON SERVICES.

"Such sounds!" Jack said.

"It is a feverish place."

"Molten!"

"You need a lie-down," the black man said.

The Welsh officer turned.

"GET BACK ON THE BORDER, JACK!"

The Welsh officer crossed the Centre quickly.

"Do you want a permanent cell?" he said.

"No."

"Then conduct yourself."

He took Jack through another gated space. A pale glow came down red stairs under white mesh. They went to the next level. White pipes ran along a yellow floor. Echoes of men came, and of squealing and slamming metal. The officer unlocked a door.

"In."

An old man smiled.

"Hello," he said. "Not bad, thank you."

Jack stood in the cell. The officer left and locked the door. Pots of water steamed on radiators. Dentures soaked by a black shoe.

"May I sit?" Jack said.

"Yes."

Jack sat.

"May I lie down?"

"Not yet."

The old man hit Jack.

"Hey!"

"Hey!"

The old man got closer.

"It's an old place," he said. "A violent place. It's all pent up, you see. In a wink of an eye. The basic is, all punishment here is bodily punishment."

The old man coughed politely into a fist and moved away.

"Most here at Pentonville are in for GBH," he said. "Rapists, drugs. Are you a rapist? Do you sell drugs?"

"No."

"What are you in here for?"

"Adultery," Jack said.

"That's no crime."

"It was for me."

The old man laughed.

"What are you here for?" Jack said.

"GBH."

"What did you do?"

"Well, it doesn't matter," he said. "Doesn't matter at all."

The old man came closer.

"Listen," he said. "A man was found behind the kitchen, he had seven holes in his head."

"O!"

"Eyes, nostrils, ears and mouth. Ha."

"Ha!"

"You're a good lad."

Jack tucked his legs under a blanket. The old man yanked it away.

"Is that a rash?" the old man said.

"Yes."

Let me see."

The old man poked Jack's leg.

"Ow!"

"Where did you get that?"

"The crematorium."

Jack ducked. The old man pounded Jack's back. The old man hit Jack with both fists.

"WOMAN!!"

The old man paced the floor, breathing hard.

"You liked that, didn't you?"

He spat on Jack. A prison officer unlocked the door. The old man backed away and pointed at Jack.

"He's pervy."

The officer turned to Jack.

"Are you?"

"No."

"Is that spit on you, Jack?" the officer said.

"Yes."

"Why?"

"I was spat upon."

The officer pointed to the old man.

"Stay against the wall."

"Sure."

The old man leaned against a wall, arms folded.

"I would like a hot plate," he said.

The officer took Jack outside and locked the door.

"Terribly sorry about this. I'll move you to a single cell," he said.

They went down the corridor. A white bannister with black rails led to a caged catwalk.

"I never grass on nobody!" the old man shouted.

They went to a different level. A white man shrieked.

"FUCK YOU!!"

"FUCK YOU!!"

The officer unlocked a cell. He opened the door.

"Bridal suite," he said.

Jack went in.

"I am claustrophobic."

"You'll be fine."

Snow fell past the black mesh windows of C Wing across a courtyard. A piece of suet dangled on a string outside the window. Pink roses grew at the exercise yard below. A shaved-headed prisoner came out of the kitchen.

"I would like a little water now, sir."

"Basin."

Jack drank, cupping hands.

"A mighty fortress is your cell, Jack."

"Is it?"

"The walls are twenty-two and a half inches thick."

"Good."

Jack sat hard on the bed.

"Lie down."

Jack lay on the bed.

"Is it soft enough, Jack?"

"Yes."

"Rest," the guard said.

"Yes."

"Yes, what?"

"I am willing," Jack said.

"Willing to do what?"

"Rest."

The officer went to the door.

"I will cage you, Jack, but I will keep you close to my heart. And you will be ordinary. You will be ordinary in an ordinary world."

"I long for it."

"I know."

Jack rolled over.

"Sometimes I am nowhere," he said. "Do you know the feeling?"

"Yes."

"What does it mean when we are nowhere?" Jack said.

"It means something else is going on."

"Are you going away?"

"For now."

"Will you close the door gently?"

"Yes."

The door closed gently. Men yelled from C Wing.

"YOU THOUGHT YOU WAS SPECIAL!"

"HEY ARE YOU LISTENING?"

Jack did a buzzard dance: one elbow up, one akimbo, head slanted, up slowly on tip toes turning.

"O . . . my baby-o . . ."

Jack turned.

". . . o, what a wicked world . . ." he said. ". . . disguised as a Fun Fair . . ."

Brilliant globules dripped from the ceiling light, burning, wobbling.

". . . it burns . . ."

Jack lay on the bed. The steel door opened. The Welsh prison officer stood in the cell. Jack sat up.

"Who are you?"

"Your jailer."

"Did I let you in?"

"No."

"How did you get in?"

"I have a key."

"Have I been sleeping?"

"Yes."

"How long have I been here?"

"I don't know. It depends who you ask. Put on your shoes. You have to testify at St. Pancras Coroner's Court."

Jack tied his shoes.

"Why?"

"You do not want a verdict of unlawful killing," the Welsh officer said.

Jack got up. They went down to the ground floor past a Visitors Room. Couples held hands across white tables. Red chairs stood at a wall. Children played. A fat prison officer sat at the rear by a black laundry bag. WANDSWORTH. They went down a long corridor toward the light of day. It was cooler. Old black manacles and a portrait of Sir Joshua Jebb hung on a wall.

Jack's clothes were folded on a chair.

"Look," the Welsh officer said. "We repaired your blazer. Couldn't get all the mud out of your trousers, though."

Jack dressed.

"Say what you will," Jack said. "I was not beset by lice."

"Track suit. In the hamper."

Jack dropped the track suit into a hamper.

"Runners?"

"On the chair."

The Welsh officer took him into a courtyard by the old execution block. It was snowing. They went up steps, a door, into a space and into a lobby. Outside, the pollarded trees stood at the high wall. Dark snow came out of a white sky. A clerk handed Jack a sheet of paper. Jack signed.

"That's it?"

"That's it."

"Where is the Coroner's Court?" Jack said.

"Down Caledonian Road, take the canal toward Kentish Town. At *The Constitution* — it's the last of old Agar Town — double back and cross the St. Pancras Road bridge. Take Granby Street and follow it to a narrow black gate in a wall. Up the steps. The Coroner's Court is on the landing."

"Cheers."

"There's a beautiful Spanish girl serving at *The Constitution*. Have a coffee."

"Will do."

"Have you money for coffee?"

"A bit short."

The clerk gave him a pound note.

"It costs a quid for a coffee?" Jack said.

"England is changed."

Jack put the note in his pocket.

"The Coroner's clerk will give you a ticket for a B&B," the clerk said.

"God bless."

Jack went out. Women walked by, heads down, scarves, small fur-lined boots. People disappeared in fog.

"How lovely they once were."

Across the road stood a Methodist chapel. It was made of yellow stock brick with orange-brick bands. One window was boarded. Stubby crosses ranged over an ochre pediment. A chimney was also yellow stock brick. Inside, straight-backed chairs with purple seats stood on an old hardwood floor, parts covered by linoleum. A green flag with tassels and a gold cross radiating triplets hung from a gold balcony. *He lives in us.* Rotted steps led to a white alms box. *How Can We Love Again?*

An African boy stopped.

"You be Christian?"

"Shouldn't think so," Jack said. "Not in the present circumstances."

The boy stared.

"I be Christian if I were you."

"Why?"

"Soon you be dead."

Jack walked down Caledonian Road. The white prison wall grew taller and the black bottom border higher as Caledonian Road sloped down. Beyond the prison a yellow café door had a sign. *There was a serious disturbance and murder outside Cally Kebab House. Did you see anything?* Turks in torn sweaters sat in the snow on a kerb eating watermelon. A red bus went by, a cylinder turning on its roof. Jack came past a building with classical pilasters that were held by black iron crossbars. Its roof was covered with sheets of plastic over planks. Welders' arcs moved in its dark basement.

Jack went down steps to the Regents Canal. A towpath headed straight toward Kentish Town. Snow stopped falling.

On the right, a red-brick wall stood in front of a brown-brick estate with white doors piled on its roof. On the left, an old basin opened. At the far end, old black warehouses had black broken windows. Behind, four cranes, two turning, rose in a silver sky over Kings Cross. Green and blue narrowboards were moored at one edge of the basin.

It was quiet. Jack walked under the Maiden Lane

bridge. A red concrete mixer crossed overhead. A swan floated below in black water. Jack looked up. The bridge struts were iced.

A round basin opened on the other side, surrounded by tangled woods. A green and white BP station was on a high bank. Narrowboats with faded gold and black diamonds bumped one another below in the green and white reflections. Jack walked the round towpath. A coot swam spreading glitter. *Griffin* moored at a locked brick shed. GOODS WAY STOP AND SHOP MOORING NO FISHING WHEN BOATERS WISH TO MOOR.

The canal narrowed. Trees leaned from both sides, rubbing, long low branches, from pink leaves and ivy. There was a sound of wing-flaps.

"O."

An unseen two-horned train bleated.

"O."

Black water glittered. *Water birds are being deliberately killed on this stretch of canal. The Police and RSPB are involved and the area is monitored.* Jack followed the canal's right angle, by a red wall hard by the towpath and the water's edge. A wire cage was embedded in the red bricks. A black cable went into a square hole. Leather-wrapped cables looped into pink-brick dusty arches. CAUTION 11,000 VOLTS. A grey boat lay under dormant willows.

"Suddenly . . . the old terror . . ."

Jack came to the St. Pancras lock.

"O."

White water poured past white stone steps to tapered

concrete bases. A white ladder went down the empty lock, dripping black algae. On the left, the black lock-master's house had black windows and trembling red geraniums. Water filled. *Sweet England* glided in under willows. Water spilled over blue irises. The gate closed behind, water lowered, *Sweet England* went out onto troubled waters.

"O."

To the right, past a horse ramp, a black gate was topped with razor spirals.

"O."

A derelict orange-brick Italianate building stood alone in a field. Black recesses ran over a black open doorway. Black-slitted arches stood under a tapered orange-brick chimney. Dark orange bands decorated light orange brick. Far away, the pink pinnacles, gold Roman numerals on a blue face of the St. Pancras Hotel clock tower rose in a bank of orange-white clouds.

There was another basin. Narrowboats were moored at a concrete wall below an electrified railroad embankment. Jack went under three bridges. It was dark. Scaffolding was at cold wet walls. WARNING BRIDGE DEMOLITION. A faded yellow tug with a dull red bottom and dusty windows, black tyres around its sides, was tied to a rusty pontoon heaped with ash. Pigeons hooted. Dust moved in a shaft of light.

Jack came out.

"The pub!"

The Constitution was high on a wall painted with cartoon narrowboats and their owners. Stella Artois umbrellas dripped in the beer garden. Jack went under a bridge and took steps back up to the road and the pub's blackboard. He went in. A beautiful Spanish girl with dyed platinum hair brought a menu.

"Coffee, luv."

"Filter?"

"What's that?"

"European."

"Is it better than instant?"

She nodded.

"All right then."

"White?"

"Black."

She went to the bar. Jack wiped his hands with a serviette.

"I sweat ammonia."

He looked around. Yellow and maroon pillars held up the bar's wood canopy. Part of the embossed ceiling sloped where it had cracked. There was an American pool table. Jack sat by a window on a carpeted platform. Outside, past the bridge, the canal turned a sharp corner toward Camden Town. Two derelicts sat on a bench.

The Spanish girl served coffee.

"Ta, luv."

Jack trembled. The cup and saucer clattered.

"Sorry."

Jack left the pound note and two ten pence coins on the table.

"For you, darling."

He went out. To the right, St. Pancras Road went

through a tunnel of bare trees to a purple night club and O'Reilly's pub. Jack went left, onto the bridge. Tops of trains moved slowly over the three bridges. *God's Dragonfly* puttered below. A young woman in a red flannel shirt and jeans leaned at the tiller bar. Jack waved. She looked away. As her boat went under the bridge she waved.

Jack came down the bridge past a grey factory with a serrated roof standing in weeds and a steel sorting office to Travis Perkins lumber and a scrap metal merchant's dark hall. Zinc glittered.

"Granby Street!"

Black carriage lamps lined the dusty street at a high hospital wall. Where the canal was visible, at a broken slat fence tangled in raspberry vines, Granby Street turned sharply. Jack went along a wall into a narrow black gate. Steps curved up to a landing.

The St. Pancras Coroner's Court was a low orange-brick chapel with a low shingled roof, black gothic windows and miniature orange-brick buttresses. Yellow chandeliers burned inside behind a partly opened blue curtain. Its brown door projected. Pink roses grew by red-leaved glossy bushes. ST. PANCRAS CORONER'S COURT. *All public enquiries to mortuary via coroner's court. Court cannot provide refreshment.*

Across the landing was a scratched steel door. ST. PANCRAS MORTUARY. FUNERAL DIRECTORS ONLY. Jack looked in a window. There was a sign. *Please ensure that your hands are clean. Please do not bring food or chewing gum. Please take care not to allow anything to touch the surface of anything. Remember not to turn the bodies over but to lift them. Always handle by the extreme edge.*

A small black ornamental gate with gold flourishes at small orange-brick buttresses led to the St. Pancras burial gardens. Huge forked trees grew over asphalt paths that wound through uneven ground. There were isolated sarcophagi. A stone urn had a stone braided linen cloth. A bird pecked at its water.

A pony-tailed coroner's clerk with a paunch, wearing a white shirt and red tie, opened the Coroner's Court door.

"Is your name Jack?"

"Yes."

"You're from the prison?"

"Yes."

"Did you stop at the *Constitution*?"

"Yes."

"Did you see the beautiful Spanish girl?"

"Yes."

"Were you thunderstruck?"

"Don't recall," Jack said. "Do you have a ticket for a B&B?"

"No."

"The prison said."

"No."

"Could you check?" Jack said.

The Coroner's clerk went inside. Jack paced the landing. A tapered translucent lamp in a black iron frame stood at the top of the stairs. An electric wire hung overhead. Jack smoked at a green punched-hole metal bench at the low landing wall. Cigarette butts lay all around.

Jack looked out where Granby Street joined Camley.

The electrified railroad embankment was topped with barbed wire tangled in white morning glory. Electric girders hung by steel poles. A green train, *Midland and Mainline*, went slowly by. Beyond, girders and poles stood upright in acres of mud. St. Pancras clock tower was far away in haze.

The Coroner's clerk came out.

"Time for court," he said.

Jack ground out a cigarette.

"No ticket?" he said.

"No."

Jack followed the clerk up two steps into a short white corridor with a green carpet. On the right was a brown door. PRIVATE. There was a second brown door. COURT.

"Will I have a jury?" Jack said.

"No."

The Coroner's clerk took a black coat off a coat rack and put it on.

"Does everybody wear black?" Jack said.

"Yes."

"Is it the law?"

"No."

A reception window behind pebbled glass stood at the end of the corridor. A silver bell was on a white sill. There was a sound of a keyboard. Men laughed.

"Is there a loo?" Jack said.

"Around the corner."

"Back in a tick."

Around the corner a constable sat in a room. He wore a black uniform with a silver chain from the breast pocket to a silver button. He did not look up. Jack went to the Gentlemen's Room. The door opened outwardly. The room was so small he squeezed in, arms first.

Jack went back.

"I didn't take too long, did I?" Jack said.

"Not at all."

The Coroner's clerk opened the Court door.

"Go in."

Jack went in. Five long pews with red leather seats faced front. White gothic windows looked past pointed plantain that wavered on raised black earth onto the burial gardens. Chandeliers burned gold-yellow. In front of the pews, two varnished tables, one with a flask, were on a hardwood floor. A two-leveled jury box had red leather seats, elaborate newel posts and black microphones. Up three green-carpeted steps with black and yellow warning strips on the edges was a blonde wood witness stand, a table with the Baghavad Gita, Old Testament, New Testament and laminated affirmation cards. A bulletin board was stuck with red push pins. The Coroner's desk was on the dais. Its chair had elaborate newel posts and stood under a coat of arms: the lion and unicorn.

"Sit."

"Where?"

"First pew."

Jack sat. A reporter for the *New Camden Journal*, wearing a trench coat, sat at the table with the flask.

"Family member?" the reporter said.

"Yes."

The reporter gave Jack a copy of the *New Camden Journal.*

"Cheers."

Jack read. *Vice groups move into Kings Cross. A shop arsonist was punched and bitten by two women over £10 shirt, bitten on both hands. A man attacked a schoolboy outside Acland Burghley school, Tufnell Park, kicked him unconscious, injuries to his eyes. Police were hunting a van.*

Jack turned a page.

Easy going tenant turned into a human torch. Tenant below thought he was deliberately making too much noise. King's Cross block of flats. Former dancer below. Victim slightly built. Classic music lover. Threw bucket of petrol over himself and tossed a match.

"Nothing about Brenda," Jack said.

Outside, an obelisk stood with four white lions and a turquoise rail. Down a small slope a black cottage stood at black ornamental gates with gold flourishes.

The Coroner's clerk pinned a map of Jack's flat onto the bulletin board. Mr. Salmon and his solicitor came in. Mr. Salmon wore a yellow shirt, maroon trousers and a black leather coat.

"Hello, Jack."

"Hi."

A clock ticked. A woman in a red dress came in. A balding man in a three-piece gray suit sat down. The Coroner's clerk opened the Coroner's door, leaned in, spoke and closed the door again. He pulled a beaded chain hanging from a brass cyliner lamp, on and off, on and off. The constable sat on a radiator at the windows. He studied his black dossier. The clerk knocked twice on the Coroner's door.

"All rise for Her Majesty's Coroner!"

Everybody stood. The Coroner came in. He had black hair combed back, black glasses on a round face. He wore a black suit. He carried a heavy leather dossier. He bowed and sat.

"Please be seated."

The Coroner opened the dossier.

"I am resuming and concluding the inquest in the death of Brenda Leigh, age 45, who died at Flat 3, 48 Mansfield Road, Kentish Town."

"Hampstead," Jack said.

The Coroner looked up.

"Who spoke?"

"I."

"You said?"

"That side of Mansfield Road is Hampstead," Jack said.

The Coroner looked at the clerk.

"NW3, sir. He's right."

The Coroner penned the correction.

"The first witness is PC Whitcomb."

PC Whitcomb went up the green steps to the witness stand. The clerk held a laminated affirmation card in front of him. PC Whitcomb held a miniature Bible between right thumb and forefinger.

"I swear to Almight God that the evidence I am about to give is the truth, the whole truth and nothing but the truth, so help me God."

The clerk put the Bible and laminated card on the table and stood by the bulletin board.

"You are — ?"

"PC Whitcomb, attached to the Kentish Town police station."

"You went to Number 48, Mansfield Road on the date in question?"

"I did."

"Why?"

"We had had two telephone calls complaining of a loud dispute. We had had such calls before with this couple but this time it seemed more serious."

"When did you arrive?"

"About 10 PM."

"In your own words, please."

"I went through a broken ochre picket gate. The flat is in one house of a row of seven such houses, and I heard loud voices coming from the flat."

"The house door was open?"

"Yes."

"Go on."

"I followed the sounds up the stairs to a landing. The flat door was also open."

"Was it forced open?"

"No."

"Could the door have been locked from the inside?" the Coroner said.

"Only if the lock had had an additional lever."

"So it could not be locked from the inside?"

"No."

"What kind of lock was it?"

"Banham," PC Whitcomb said. "The door locks when it is closed, with a latch."

"Go on."

"I went in. The shouts came from the bathroom which is off the bedroom."

"Can you show us on the map?"

"Yes."

PC Whitcomb went to the bulletin board. The clerk stepped aside. PC Whitcomb pointed to the map of the bathroom off the bedroom. He came back to the witness stand.

"I saw three men, the landlord and two scaffold lads, banging at the door. One part of a towel hung from the door knob. The other part was tied to a leg of the dresser in the bedroom."

"Had it been cut?"

"No. Torn."

"A frayed towel?"

"Yes."

"But it had connected the dresser to the door knob?" the Coroner said.

"Yes."

"Keeping Brenda Leigh inside?"

"Yes."

"Show us."

PC Whitcomb pointed to the dresser at the corner of the bedroom and then at the bathroom door.

"And the towel was that long?"

"Yes. It may have stretched."

Jack looked up. Two triangular skylights were embedded in a bright red ceiling. Delicate white struts went into a black slit.

Rain burst through the forked trees. It was getting dark. The obelisk gleamed. Spongy ground glittered. Water flew from the four lions and turquoise rail. Cars outside the gates had headlights on, beams sparkling in rain.

"Was the bathroom door locked?"

"No. Brenda had fallen against it. The door opened inwardly. She was very heavy and the men could not dislodge her."

"Was it slippery?" the Coroner said.

"Yes."

"Why?"

"The blood."

"Tell us about the blood."

"It was coming under the door, around our shoes," PC Whitcomb said. "When the top half of the door broke we reached down and dislodged the lady and then shoved the lower half open. Unfortunately, it slid her across the tiles on the blood and she ended at the bathtub with her face over the edge. She was still clutching the shattered medicine cabinet. There was blood on the toilet, blood on the basin, blood on the wall."

"ALL THE BLOOD IN ENGLAND!" Jack shouted.

Jack rubbed the edge of the pew.

"Was it a scene of a violence?" the Coroner said.

"Yes."

Outside, two Africans went by in the burial gardens. They held umbrellas and laughed. A German shepherd gambolled among the sarcophagi.

"Was she alive?"

"Barely."

"And you called for an ambulance?"

"No."

The Coroner looked up.

"Why not?"

"There was an ambulance strike. The landlord and scaffold fellows carried her to the Royal Free on what was left of the door."

The Coroner smiled.

"Really?"

"Yes, sir."

"I have never heard of that."

"It was only a few blocks away."

The Coroner tried not to smile. So did PC Whitcomb.

"I gave chase to her common-law husband," PC Whitcomb said. "I lost him in the Gospel Oak estates."

Jack stood.

"May it please the court —"

"Sit down."

Jack sat.

"You will have your chance to testify," the Coroner said.

"Yes, sir."

A bird pecked at a window. The coroner turned to PC Whitcomb.

"Was there evidence of drugs or alcohol?" the Coroner said.

"Fosters. Under the bed."

"Full?"

"Empty."

"Were any drugs found?"

"There were two large bottles of paracetamol and Aspirin, 325 milligrams."

"Ordinary pain killers."

"Yes."

"Full or empty?"

PC Whitcomb looked into his black dossier.

"Doesn't say."

The Coroner made a notation. He nodded to PC Whitcomb. PC Whitcomb left the witness stand.

"This concludes the testimony of PC Whitcomb," the Coroner said. "Mr. Salmon."

The *New Camden Journal* reporter yawned. Mr. Salmon took the oath.

"He's not a Christian!" Jack said.

The coroner paused.

"What is your occupation, Mr. Salmon?"

"Property."

"What was your relation to Brenda Leigh?"

"I was her landlord."

"Tell us what happened."

"It was a lovely evening," Mr. Salmon said. "The Fun Fair was on and I went there. As I went home I came to Mansfield Road."

"What time was this?"

"I should say about 9:45."

Jack stood

"Sit."

Jack sat.

"Go on."

"I heard Brenda yelling. It was her but it did not sound human. I went in and as there was no answer, opened the flat door. Landlords may do that in an emergency. I knocked on the bedroom door. There was no answer. I saw blood running under the bathroom door."

"Was the door tied with a towel?"

"Yes."

"It was frayed?"

"It must have been one of theirs. '

"What did you do?"

"I tore it off but I could not budge the door. Brenda had fallen against it. Two scaffold lads climbed in through a window."

"At that hour?"

"I pay well."

"And you, the two scaffold lads and PC Whitcomb finally knocked half the door in and shoved the bottom half open, sending her across the bathroom tiles?"

"Strangely, I do not remember PC Whitcomb." Mr. Salmon said. "Her husband came later, running in circles. I slapped him and he ran away. I believe he threw up on the stairwell. My recollection is that it was then that the constable came and gave chase."

"How did Brenda Leigh look when you broke in?"

"She was huddled, holding the medicine cabinet, which

she must have torn off the wall. Her black hair was oddly tufted by the blood. Like a doll. The kind we used to call —"

Mr. Salmon looked around.

"— picaninnies —"

Mr. Salmon made a gesture of pulling his hair up in tufts.

"I see."

The Coroner looked to Mr. Salmon's solicitor.

"Any questions?"

The solicitor stood.

"Can you describe the medicine cabinet?" he said.

"It was a standard bathroom medical cabinet, firmly attached by four butterfly bolts at each corner," Mr. Salmon said. "It had black diamonds along the edges of the mirror. A crystal knob. About six inches deep."

"With glass shelves?" the solictor said.

"Yes."

"Where did you purchase the medicine cabinet?"

"At Queen's Crescent market."

"Was it heavy?"

"No. Ten pounds, I should reckon."

"A weight of ten pounds, secured in four places, is normally sufficient to hold, is it not?"

"I am not a builder but I believe, yes, it would," Mr. Salmon said.

"So it could not have come off easily?"

"No."

"Or by itself?"

"Never."

"There was no defect of workmanship?" the solicitor said.

"None."

"Could it be ripped off the wall?"

"Only in a frenzy," Mr. Salmon said.

The solicitor sat.

"Your testimony is concluded, Mr. Salmon," the Coroner said. "You may stay or leave, as you wish."

Mr. Salmon and his solicitor left. A squall blew over the sarcophagi. Plantain beat wildly at the windows. Twigs sprayed water. It was 4:30. It was dark. Gold-red glowed on a sarcophagus from the chandeliers.

"Dr. Levin, please."

Dr. Levin took the oath. He wore tortoise shell glasses and his head was nearly bald. He wore a light grey suit and wide blue tie. He carried a manila folder.

"I am Dr. Brian Levin. I am an internist at the Royal Free Hospital and was on call on the night. I certified the death of Brenda Leigh."

"What happened?"

"At about 11 PM a woman, about 45 or 50, obese, was brought to A&E on a broken door. She was bleeding profusely, wrapped in sheets and a blanket. She was wearing a black miniskirt and fishnet stockings. Rather odd for a woman of her build. Her hair was tufted, sticky with blood. It had also been dyed red. Her face was white. She had a very unusual expression. A sort of a pucker."

"For a kiss?"

"Hate."

"Hate?"

"One does not kiss for love like that," Dr. Levin said.

"You checked her heart?"

"Asystolic."

Dr. Levin read.

"Lacerations abundant at the shoulders, upper arms and left jaw. Part of the right eye was burst. I cut her clothes off. Some shards of the mirror were still in her. Lacerations also on her upper thighs and hips. By themselves, the lacerations were not life threatening but all together, they were to prove fatal. The pulse was irregular and slowing down. She was not breathing. She suffered two seizures and was not expected to survive."

"Did you attempt to remove the shards?" the Coroner said.

"There was no time."

"Did you try to resuscitate her?"

"We gave her blood transfusions. I used a Brooks Airway and external cardiac massage," Dr. Levin said. "The crash team came but by then her eyes had shut. They applied shock but there was no movement. She was intubated with 100 percent oxygen and given more shock plus intracardial adrenalin. I pronounced her life-extinct at 10 minutes past midnight."

Jack jumped up.

"They killed her!"

"There was no life in her!" Dr. Levin said.

"O!"

"She was dead!"

"She was not!" Jack said.

"*Completely!!*"

"The Royal Free could have saved her!"

"How?"

"Surgery!"

"There was no *time* for surgery!"

The Coroner leaned toward Jack.

"If you have a grievance, take it up with the hospital. If they give you no satisfaction you are entitled to make arrangements to have the hospital's conduct investigated."

"The Royal Free will cover it up!" Jack said. "You know they will!"

"You can sue."

"I can't afford it!"

"Contact Camden Services."

"Where is my B&B ticket?" Jack said.

"I know nothing about your ticket. Sit."

Jack sat. It got quiet. The Coroner leaned forward.

"This is not a trial," he said. "It is a Coroner's Court. We are here to determine the facts of death. Much as I would regret it, as would you, I can remove you from the court. I am sensitive to your distress but I will not have the court interrupted. I can adjourn for fifteen minutes so you can recover."

"No."

"Very well."

Lights went by. Pools shivered at the sunken bases of sarcophagi.

"We waited one hour," Dr. Levin said, "and then moved her to the hospital morgue."

"Did you wait to see if the monitors would show life?"

"There is a tradition at the Royal Free that the soul lingers an hour after death."

"Really?"

"Yes."

"I did not know that."

"An old tradition."

Dr. Levin smiled. He left. The Coroner looked at a typed report.

"I have here a copy of the toxicologist's report," he said. "Brenda Leigh's alcohol content was .462. Is that toxic, Mr. Newberry?"

"If she had not been an alcoholic she would have died of it," the clerk said.

"Was there not an addendum to the report?" the Coroner said.

"It was sent to the wrong address and can not be retrieved."

"Thank you. I shall include the report as Document C-1 under Rule 37 of the *Coroner's Rules.*"

The Coroner looked up.

"Mrs. Stuart."

Mrs. Stuart was short, with black hair and glasses. She wore a red dress over which she had put a tweed coat. She came to the witness stand, opened a report, leaned forward, took the oath and tapped the microphone.

"I am Mrs. Mary Stuart," she said. "I am an officer of the St. Pancras Coroner's Court. I have read the post-mortem as submitted by Dr. Freddy Patel."

She looked down at the report.

"The body was examined in autopsy at the St. Pancras

morgue," she said. "The brain was sent to Queen's Hospital neuropathology."

"THE BRAIN?!"

Jack twisted.

"O HORROR!"

"Go on."

"The brain showed a degree of cortical atrophy," Mrs. Stuart read. "That is, the brain was hardened. The liver was with fatty tissue. Both are consistent with heavy drinking. Her heart was enlarged, also consistent with heavy drinking, and the transverse artery was 90 percent closed. There was a poorly healed fracture of the right arm. Minor skin lesions. Lymph and endocrine systems normal. The rest of the body system unremarkable. Some bacteria, consistent with alcohol and death."

"Dr. Levin told us about the lacerations."

Mrs. Stuart looked again at the report.

"Also, mercury flakes," she said.

"Mercury?"

"From the cabinet mirror."

"Interesting."

The Coroner noted the mercury flakes.

"Were there any gashes of the wrist?" he asked.

"No."

"Dr. Patel's cause of death?"

"*Exsanguination.*"

"That was the cause of death arrived at in the opening of the inquest."

"Yes."

Mrs. Stuart left.

"That concludes the autopsy report submitted by Dr. Freddy Patel," the Coroner said. "I shall include it as Document C-2 under Rule 37 of the *Coroner's Rules*."

He looked up.

"Jack."

"Yes?"

"Are you ready to testify?"

"Every Christian ought to testify."

Jack went up the three steps to the witness stand. The clerk pointed to the holy books and laminated cards on the table.

"Which one, Jack?"

Jack pointed to a laminated card. *Affirmation if no religious beliefs.*

"You said you were Christian."

WWhat a Christian says when he is not a Christian may or may not be normal. Nevertheless, it is true."

The clerk stood behind Jack and held the laminated card around in front of him.

"I," the clerk said.

"I."

"Do solemnly, sincerely and truly declare —"

"Solemnly and truly declare."

"That evidence touching this matter —"

"Evidence of the matter."

"Will be the truth, the whole truth and nothing but the truth."

"I do."

"No. Swear and affirm."

"Swear and affirm."

The clerk looked at the Coroner.

"Good enough," the Coroner said.

The clerk stood at the bulletin board. Jack leaned over the witness stand to look at the Coroner.

"I am pleased to give whatever talents I may possess," Jack said, "to further the cause of the working class."

"Thank you."

"Pleasure."

"Is your name Jack Russell?"

"It is Jack. I do not know about the Russell."

The Coroner read his dossier. People waited. Railroad brakes squealed over the burial gardens,

"You were recently released from prison?"

"Yes."

"Have you ever been a patient at a mental facility?"

"No."

The Coroner flexed his fingers and picked up his pen.

"May it please the court —" Jack said.

"Quiet."

The Coroner put down his pen.

"You were the last to see Brenda Leigh alive, Jack" he said.

"I know."

"And you had had an argument."

"Yes."

"What about?"

"When you are in a state it does not matter," Jack said.

The Coroner studied Jack.

"Jack, you are not required to say anything under oath that might incriminate you. Are you aware of that?"

"O, yes. I know all about that."

"Do you?"

"No. May I be excused?"

"No."

The Coroner pursed his lips.

"How well did you know your wife, Jack?'

"She did predate on me."

"Was she suicidal?"

"Well, she never threw herself under the Northern Line," Jack said. "As far as I know."

"But she was depressed?"

"She did not want to live."

"Why did you tie her in the bathroom?" the Coroner said.

"I was on a mission," Jack said.

"Where did you go?"

"The Fun Fair."

"On Hampstead Heath?"

"Yes, sir. On Hampstead Heath. The Fun Fair."

"Why?"

"Everybody goes to the Fun fair."

"Do they?"

"Bright lights and all. Loudspeakers. Cotton candy. Lots of cotton candy."

Jack drank from a cup of water. A telephone rang in a far office. Nobody answered.

"Did you meet someone?" the Coroner said.

"No."

"No?"

"She was not there," Jack said.

"Why not?"

Jack drank more water.

"She did not exist."

"So you could not have met her?"

"Whether she existed or not," Jack said, "she was not there."

Jack held out his cup. The clerk poured more water.

"Jack?"

"Yes?"

"You had expectations?"

"Certainly."

"Of what?"

"God appeared in the human form," Jack said.

"It was a failed seduction."

"Yes."

"You wanted to be in love."

"Yes."

"But sin was most active," the Coroner said.

"The temperature was very high, sir."

"Well, then?"

"Evil," Jack said, "is most intense when one is in love."

"I was not aware of that."

"Nobody but me could cross a shame bridge," Jack said.

He spread his arms and turned to the pews.

"Can I get a witness?!"

"You *are* the witness!"

"I have nothing more to say."

"Then this concludes your testimony," the Coroner said.

Jack bowed.

"This concludes my testimony," he said.

The clerk took Jack back to the front pew. The Coroner stood.

"All rise for Her Majesty's Coroner!"

The Coroner bowed. The clerk opened the door to the Coroner's study. The Coroner went in. The door closed. People left and milled in the corridor or smoked outside.

"Hey!"

Jack ran after the clerk.

"Clerk!" he shouted. "Where is the B&B?!"

"SOD YOUR TICKET!"

"Where do I sleep?

"Out there!"

Jack went out. The sky was black. A white van hit a black car's rear on the road below the obelisk. The drivers argued. Jack went back into the court. People waited for the Coroner. The clerk knocked twice on the Coroner's door.

"All rise for Her Majesty's Coroner!"

Everybody stood. The Coroner came in, slightly hunched, with his dossier. He bowed.

"Please be seated."

Everybody sat. The Coroner opened his dossier.

"This concludes the inquest into the death of Brenda Leigh," he said. "I am satified that this was the body of Brenda Leigh who grew up in Mile End and died at 48 Mansfield Road NW3.

"PC Whitcomb testified that he was called to 48 Mansfield Road where he found men banging on the bathroom door from which Brenda Leigh's blood flowed. Brenda was firmly lodged inside the door and as she was heavy they could not open it. She was dislodged and when the men shoved the lower part of the door she slid across the floor tiles and came to rest face down at the bathtub.

"Dr. Brian Levin testified that despite valiant efforts her life could not be saved. She was pronounced life-extinct at the Royal Free 10 minutes past midnight. We accepted a summary of the toxicologist's report which indicated that Brenda Leigh was highly intoxicated. Paracetamol and Aspirin were found in the flat but did not show in the autopsy. Mrs. Stuart, an officer of this court, read a summary of the post-mortem submitted by Dr. Freddy Patel which confirmed the preliminary cause of death as *exsanguination*. There was no evidence of third party involvement. There were no witnesses.

"The standard of evidence for a verdict of suicide is *beyond reasonable doubt*. I am not satisfied that a verdict of suicide is beyond reasonable doubt. On balance of probability she died of an accident to which alcohol contributed. Brenda Leigh may have taken out her self-loathing or her rage against her husband by smashing her image in the medicine cabinet mirror and ripping it off the wall, or clutched it as she slipped and fell on it, driving many small but ultimately fatal shards into her body.

"I note the suspicious circumstances of a towel that was used by Brenda Leigh's common-law husband to tie her in but I am satisfied he was on a mission of lust disguised as religious experience."

Jack stood.

"A wound that will not stanch!"

"Sit *down*!"

Jack sat. The clerk stood behind him. The Coroner drank a glass of water with a trembling hand. He read.

"I am satisfied that this was the body of Brenda Leigh. I am satisfied that she was born at Mile End, London. I am satisfied that she died of *exsanguination*."

The Coroner closed the dossier.

"I am satisfied."

He banged the gavel.

"Open verdict."

The Coroner stood.

"All rise for Her Majesty's Coroner!"

Everybody stood. The Coroner bowed. The clerk opened the Coroner's door and the Coroner went in. The door closed. Jack went out. It was cold. Bright wire baskets of purple petunias swayed in the chapel light. White Dusty Miller shivered in black earth. Mrs. Stuart left in her red car below the landing wall.

Jack opened the burial garden gate. He stepped over a plywood sheet into the burial grounds.

"GOD WHAT HAVE I DONE!!"

Rain spattered.

"O!"

Sarcophagi gleamed.

"O!"

Dark maroon hospital blocks rose from below a retaining wall behind the dripping forked trees of the burial gardens. Yellow room lights gleamed. Black fire escapes zig-zagged down in dark brick recesses. Two orange-brick chapels stood at angles on an asphalt court. Black rods kept maroon hospital buildings apart in a narrow alley. From the asphalt a flare-bottomed smokestack rose into rapidly moving white silver-edged clouds.

"O!"

Jack whirled.

"Effaced! *Effaced!* EFFACED!"

A light went off in the Coroner's study. The court was dark. The sharp plantain on raised black earth glistened at the gothic windows. Jack stumbled past the Coroner's study. A white balustrade curved around white stone steps that led down to white rubble. Jack bumped into a rusted grave rail. A black locomotive moved over a green construction wall, past a tree whose roots were above ground and packed with tombstones.

"O!"

Leaves, unseen, scuttled in the dark.

"LEAVES! FLYING!"

Vapour rose.

"O!"

Jack stumbled over the uneven ground, crushing daffodil husks. Mud sucked his shoes. Lights moved.

"LIGHTS! YELLOW!"

A church bell tolled.

"Eh?"

A haloed moon glided out over the Old St. Pancras Parish Church. Its clock had gold Roman numerals under a black iron filigreed vane.

The church's windows were black-meshed. Effaced

white plaques studded a rough stone wall. A cage of tilted sarcophagi in wet brown leaves projected at the rear. At the front, a heavy black bolt-studded wood door had multiple stone surrounds: stone balls, diagonals, spirals, wavy stone lines.

A Death Lady in a long black gown and wide black-brimmed hat, wearing red lipstick, rattled the door.

"But you see, darling?" she said. "The church is locked!"

Jack recoiled backward down the entry path. A sarcophagus had a lying stone figure with a broken head. He went down broadening steps through a black ornamental gate to the road. CTL were shoring up the Midland Railway viaduct past a purple-leaved Japanese maple that leaned out of the burial gardens. Floodlights buzzed and snapped. Pile-driving rods stood in glowing orange and white tubs on sparkling sand. A generator throbbed. An orange ditch-digger's headlights moved under acetylene lights.

"My eyes!"

A piledriver slammed rods.

"My ears!"

He ran to the Brill, a dark area under three trestle bridges that came together over brick supports. One orange globe gleamed in a four-globe night light. A bush grew out of a wall. Ferns dripped under the bolted bridge bottoms. Pigeons fluttered at wet walls. Black leaves that grew out of black vents rose and fell. Electric wires ran along steel plates. A locomotive headlight swept the Brill. Something enormous and heavy rumbled overhead, slowly pushing water through the boats.

"O, the abomination . . ."

The piledriver echoed.

"O."

Two lads looking for trouble came toward the Brill.

"Look!

"Where?"

"In the Brill! The guy with the silver lapels!"

Jack scuttled out of the Brill onto a white road under an unhaloed moon in a pure black sky. Nothing moved. An enormous crystalline half-completed steel platform glittered. Across the road, black arches in doublets, triplets and singles lined an old red-orange viaduct closer to King's Cross. Black shadows of light poles fell in three directions. Jack sneaked into a vault. There was a smell of tyres. Electric cables and copper piping lined curved walls. A soaked mattress leaned against a locked cage. FULLY ALARMED. NO CASH. PALLETS WANTED. Africans in yellow rubber boots hosed and sponged a Mercedes. One looked up.

"You're lost, mate."

"Can I sleep in the vaults?" Jack said.

"Wouldn't."

"Then where?"

"Try behind Kings Cross station. Someone might take you in."

"Cheers."

Jack went out the other side of the viaduct vaults. Shops were embedded in the arches. A pewter stag stood on a pine table. Ceramic tiles were on display. Valves and rods were on a yellow table. *Brake Fluid The Hidden Danger.* There was an office. *Asian Funeral Directors, washing and dressing facilities, serving families of all faiths, Saturday and Sunday funerals, memorial flowers, funeral plans.*

Across the road in the rain, Kings Cross railway station stood, yellow-grey stock brick with floodlights brightening two flat wings and an enormous round-top black window under a stubby Italianate tower capped with a four-sided clock with black Roman numerals, topped by an iron filigree weather vane. A pit had been dug, lined with cables, boards that stuck up from rubble. Electric lights gleamed on yellow ropes folded on scaffolding below street level.

Jack crossed the road, through a row of black taxis, passed a cylinder that protruded through the road from the Underground, and went behind Kings Cross station to the Great Northern Hotel. The *Great Northern Bar* and *Great Northern Coffee House* were bright and busy. People looked out at Jack. Jack threw mud.

"I'M NOT FILTHY!"

A row of black two-up, two-down houses was derelict. Shards of glass covered empty floors. A wire hung over a free-standing iron door. Across a muddy road, past black gas rings, was the BP station over the black canal.

Jack fell to one knee.

"Hey!"

An old man waved from a balcony. He wore a long-sleeved white undershirt and grey trousers rolled to his knees.

"Is this a hostel?" Jack said.

"Yes."

"Run by Camden Council?"

"Yes."

Jack folded his arms, shivering.

"Can I come in?"

"Sure! Come to my room. Have trout with me."

Jack stepped over bricks to the hostel door. Newspapers were stuck inside its glass. A young man polished the knobs. A bell hop, a skinny old man with a sunken chest, sandy-red hair and freckles, in a red jacket with gold buttons and tan trousers, leaned at a counter where umbrellas stood out of an elephant's foot. Ornate woodwork was being varnished. Two pillars stood with spiral capitals. Balconies surrounded a sunken floor with a drain. DHSS men climbed stairs. An NHS locum came down. Jack and the old man bumped through old men who crowded the lobby.

"What's your name?"

"Jack."

Jack climbed.

"What's yours?"

"O, a little of this and a little of that."

They climbed.

"Lots of stairs, eh?" the old man said.

"Yes."

"It used to be for German artisans," the old man said. "They've gone. The Germans. We're still here. For now."

Jack and the old man went along the mezzanine into a corridor with green flocked wallpaper and beige baseboards. Old men in boxer shorts carried empty burlap bags. A linen closet was open. A pile of thin grey blankets and white pillows lay on yellow shelves. Farther down, cut garments hung on a wall. Around a corner, a naked man washed in a communal shower.

He looked up and covered his private parts.

"Get lost."

"Take it easy."

"I'll call the police."

They turned another corner.

"In."

Jack went in. A bed had a bedspread with cigarette burns. There was a sign. SOFT BED. Snoopy and Rupert Bear lay on a pillow. The old man closed the door behind and locked it. A pepper plant was on a night table. Union Jacks were clipped to a clothes line from wall to wall.

"Comfy," Jack said.

"I was lucky."

A man cried behind the wall.

"*LOST! LOST! WHERE ARE ME SONS!*"

"What's wrong?" the old man said.

"Heard something," Jack said. "It was frightening."

"Are you sure?"

"Yes."

"I am here, though.

"You are."

"And that is all you need."

There was a seascape.

"Ramsgate?"

"Margate."

Water dripped.

"Faucet?" Jack said.

"Rain."

"But there are four floors above us," Jack said.

"One man's floor is another man's ceiling."

"May I use the loo?" Jack said.

"Sure."

The loo was through the kitchen. Jack tested the door. It opened outwardly. Black vents were in the floor. There was no basin. He read the *Islington Journal. Killing of Ellen, 90. Worst fears on drug estate. Fear has spread through our elderly community. Stabbed 50 times and throat slit early Friday. Her home was at Great Croft, Crown Street, King's Cross. The elderly are in the same building as drug addicts, mentally ill and alcoholics. Four months earlier a retired draughtsman, Angus Gilmour, 63, was dowsed with petrol and set alight in nearby Tonbridge Street, King's Cross. The accused woman is now standing trial at the Old Bailey. "I have not slept in my bed for more than a year," the old woman said. "I can't live with it, the fear."*

"Wash your hands."

"Where?"

"Kitchen."

Jack washed at the kitchen basin. There was a poster of a Coca-Cola bottle. Jack rubbed his gums with his forefinger and gargled. The old man sat on the bed.

"Look at your shoes, my friend," he said. "You come to God's world and this is what you leave with."

"If that."

"And that stupid blazer."

The old man pointed to a straight-backed chair by the bed.

"Come to the bedroom."

Jack went to the bedroom.

"Sit."

Jack sat.

"Take your shoes off," he said.

"Why?"

"The floor is soft."

"Is it?"

The old man took off Jack's shoes.

"Now feel your feet on the floor. Doesn't that feel good?"

"It does!"

"Sit on the bed," the old man said.

"May I?"

"Of course."

Jack sat on the bed.

"Lie down."

Jack lay on the bed.

The old man turned off the light.

"It's dark," Jack said.

"O, I see like Bartolomeus."

"What are you doing?" Jack said.

"Lying down, too."

"Why?"

"So we can have sex."

"TURN ON THE LIGHT!!"

The old man flapped around and flicked on the light.

"Ever had sex?"

"Once."

"Yes. I can see it has marked you," the old man said.

Jack sat up.

"Tea?" the old man said.

"Lovely."

The old man went to the kitchen and brought back a Coronation Cup. It was gold-painted on the handle and showed George V in a blue military uniform with a red sash and white ribbons, and Queen Mary in a white dress with a blue sash.

"What about your cup?" Jack said.

"I have a Cadbury's cup."

The old man boiled water.

"Toffees?"

"Do you have some?"

"Wouldn't offer if I didn't."

The old man took a grey box of red-ribboned cellophane-wrapped toffees from a drawer. He brought out cream and sugar and poured hot water through tea leaves into a strainer and into Jack's mug.

"Where are you from, Jack?"

"Not sure."

"Have you had ECT?"

"No."

"Ever had a lobotomy?"

"No."

"Did you kill somebody?" he said.

"No."

"I'll bet you did."

The old man turned at the kitchen door.

"Trout?"

"Can I?" Jack said.

"I invited you."

The old man went back into his galley kitchen. He lighted the grill and blew a blue flame down a row of gas holes.

"Sweet and fresh! What more could you want?" he called. "You can't get this everywhere. Usually you don't get the good kind. I'll never serve croissants, though."

Suddenly he went to a window.

"O, a Lebanese!"

"Where?"

"Out the window."

Jack went to the window. The old man went back to the grill.

"He's gone," Jack said.

"Could have been a Lebanese," the old man said. "Look! White eyes!"

"The Lebanese?"

"The trout. Sit."

Jack sat at a brown and white checked oilcloth-covered table. The old man served trout and buttered new potatoes.

"Mm."

"Ah."

"Nice."

Jack sucked fish bones.

"I know nothing, Jack. Nothing. I don't even know what I know. A sinister racket is going on."

"The Brill is gone," Jack said.

"For now."

He finished the new potatoes.

"This is a conversation," Jack said. "Isn't it?"

"Yes."

"I thought so," Jack said.

"Look!" the old man said. "A girl!"

"Where?"

"Down below. On the street."

"A sex object?" Jack said.

"No. A very decent lass."

"Than we'll let her be," Jack said.

The old man brought a bottle of Jack Daniels.

"American!"

They drank.

"The Channel Tunnel!" Jack said.

"Right."

"Section via Stratford, East London to St. Pancras! 330 kilometres per hour! Four stations, one underground at Midland Road!"

"Headlights!"

"Speed!"

"Dynamism!"

"NO MORE WORKING CLASS!"

"NO MORE REALITY!"

"WHOO!"

"WHOO!"

They drank.

"Crap."

"Crap."

They finished the bottle. The old man playfully

punched Jack.

"Hey."

"Ow!"

The old man rubbed trout in Jack's hair.

"HEY!"

Jack fell to the floor. He pointed at the old man.

"You!"

"Me!"

"You were in the prison!"

"You're *still* in prison!"

"I am not!"

The old man spread margarine into the fish bones. He slapped Jack.

"WOMAN!"

"I am not!"

"YOU WISH YOU WERE!"

"I can't believe you said that!"

"Well, I did."

Jack crawled.

"You're not the boss of the world!" he said.

"I am."

"Not."

"*Your* world!"

"O dreadful beast! "

"I am Boss of the World! So wake up, Jack! WAKE UP!"

He punched Jack.

"My tooth!"

"SOD YOUR TOOTH!"

Jack got up.

"O," the old man said. "He fights back."

The old man back-pedalled like a drunken boxer and waved his fists.

"No more panty hose for you!" he said.

Jack kicked him in the stomach. The old man knocked him against the door. Jack unlocked the door and ran into the corridor. The old man tackled him. Jack crawled toward the stairwell. The old man rode on Jack's back.

"DONKEY!"

The old man dug his heels into Jack's sides.

"GIDDYUP!"

Jack rotated down the stairs. The old man fell off and waved his arms on the mezzanine.

"I AM THE VOICE OF EXPERIENCE!!"

Jack ran through the lobby. Old men cheered.

"PEOPLE LIKE YOU ARE EASY TO ERADICATE!"

Jack stumbled past the Great Northern Hotel to Kings Cross station.

"Help!"

People crowded under a green awning. Luggage went by. A suitcase burst. An African blushed.

"Things fall apart," he apologised.

A man pointed to Kings Cross's clock tower. It was very late.

"I told you!"

A bird flew, one wing up, one wing down, into the St. Pancras Roman numerals. It fell turning. Headlights came around a big curve from Grays Inn Road past a flat-iron building with a lighthouse on top. Shops were shuttered where Pentonville Road separated from Euston Road and Caledonian Road ended. *Chicken Kebab. Eastern Eye, Dress World. Mole Jazz. Chop Chop Noodle Bar.* He went down into an underground lavatory. He washed his hands. His lip was split. He combed the trout out of his hair with his fingers.

"I should have kicked him harder."

Up on Euston Road, taxi brakes squealed. Lorries honked. A driver leaned out.

"Watch where you're going!

"Sod off!"

Across Euston, behind a slender tree that grew from a sidewalk grate, a small white police station with blue trim stood in the rain. Its mirrorized window was blank. There was a security panel and black iron steps led down to a basement. KEEP GATE LOCKED AT ALL TIMES. Drops flew from the shaking leaves. Next door, *Ladbroke's* steamed yellow, its black floor littered with butts. Dogs raced on a monitor. Night mist blended into blue and pink wraparound neon. *Play to Win.*

"Where is the damn girl?"

Jack went down Birkenhead Street. Bright signs hung out from black iron hotel balconies. Kings Cross Methodist Church's huge ochre pediment was stained with rain-fingers. Razor wire led to a cobbled lane. Dripping ferns were under a pub sign. *Guardian Angel.*

Jack went in. Etched mirrors hung on flocked wallpaper. Between them were prints of *Paternoster Row*, the *Cheshire Cheese*, *Westminster Abbey at Night.* Pink floral lamps rose in brass sconces. There was a wood fire.

Women sat at varnished iron-legged tables and laughed. Crepes Florentine were served. Kirs royale made the rounds. Gold-red firelight glinted on brandy snifters. The publican escorted him out.

"Is she here?"

"Who?" the publican said.

"Who I am looking for."

"No."

The publican went in. An armless beggar, eyes wide, opened his mouth, a black hole: *Nowhere!* At the Russell Hotel a bus boy came out carrying a tub of dirty dishes. NO SEEING. A waiter came out, uncorking a wine bottle. NO HEARING. The cashier came out, counting change. NO SMELLING. The chef came out. He sharpened his knife. NO TASTING. A woman came down, opening a white umbrella. NO TOUCHING. Past an orange-brick estate, opposite a dark church, a Muslim woman stood in a bright pharmacy with her son. *O, the death that you will die.*

Pearly sparkling layers of mist crossed Charing Cross Road. Buses went by, shaking leaves. People left theatres. Black taxis went away.

St. Martin's-in-the-Field's lighted up.

"O."

Bright fluted columns, black on the inside, held up a porch. *Ich Dien.* Black carriage lamps hung over three brown doors. *2:15 PM Chinese Service. 5 PM Chorale Evensong.* Stained glass was dark. Pocked stone steps broadened to Charing Cross. There was a black ornamental gate and black iron fence. Its black spindles had black iron balls. The steeple was bright with narrowing black slits.

A green arch lighted up.

"A green arch!"

"What is your name?"

Jack went down the steps. He knocked at a black door under a light. *The Connection.* The door opened.

"Are you beset with lice?"

"No."

"Come in."

Jack went in. Derelicts crowded a room. The floor and walls were scuffed yellow. Hot lamps steamed. Bedrolls, wet jackets hung from pegs. *Every Day Is Judgment Day.* Chairs were set up in groups. Blurred faces moved. Men metamorphosed. Far away, an eating room had a flickering television. Jack sat on a chair under an incandescent lamp.

A derelict pushed him off.

"That's my chair."

"It's my chair," Jack said.

The derelict grabbed it.

"MY CHAIR!!"

Jack grabbed the chair and swung it. The derelict ducked but fell.

"Okay," he said. "But I will get you."

Jack slumped on the chair and bent forward, holding his head.

". . . the choirs . . ."

His arm trembled to the floor.

". . . in my head . . ."

He fell.

"Jack!"

"Mm?"

"Get up!"

Jack's right hand twitched.

"I shall be with you presently," he said. "Though in some ways I am already gone."

A church worker hauled Jack to the door, opened it, pushed Jack onto the steps and slammed the door.

"No sleeping on the floor," he said.

Jack stood in the rain.

"O."

Trafalgar sparkled. It was late night at the National Gallery. The gallery was symmetrical on the outside, but asymetrical inside. Its black cupola was in a pink cloud. The porch's floor had a black and white serpentine. Classical statues of women stood in niches. The porch ceiling had mirrored squares. A classical horse and rider were over an oversized dark doorway that led past the floodlights. Down the long iron fence of a wing was a banner: *Titian: Noli Me Tangere.*

He looked up.

"Ah. English rain."

He opened his mouth.

"Thank you."

St. Martin's night market lighted up. Tie-dye T-shirts, pub signs, red jester hats, ties with Underground maps, the Queen's picture, petit-point change purses, embroidered photo albums, ceramic Churchills, wind chimes, Egyptian papyrus and onyx glittered. Blue and white pinwheels spun. Chinese scrolls spiraled up and down in a breeze. Jade Buddhas smiled. Pennants snapped.

A stall table covered by white linen lighted up.

"*My* stall!"

Jack ran behind, picked up a bell and rang it.

"Merry bells!"

The vestry hall lighted. *Hail the Glory Dawning.* Light shot from the crypt. Jack clapped his hands.

"*O glory!!*"

Church bells rang.

"O!"

A young woman with gold-red hair, wearing a thin salmon sweater with a thin gold chain and a blue-grey skirt, stepped down from the National Gallery porch past the Titian banner to the night market.

"What are your selling?" she said.

Jack looked down at the boxes on the linen.

"Old prints, love."

"Yes. That's a Noel Rooke."

She leaned forward and her slender fingers pulled prints forward in the boxes, one by one.

"You like old prints, don't you?"

"Yes."

"Sure. Everybody does."

He stepped back.

"You have pretty earrings," he said.

Wisps of gold-red hair trembled in the night breeze at the back of her neck.

"But these are facsimiles," she said.

"O, no."

"I am afraid so. Cut from books."

She looked up at Jack. Light came into her green eyes' edges. Birds exploded from a tree. Jack backed further away.

"Everything in front of you, my sweetheart, is genuine."

She put prints back.

"How is Ludmilla?" he said.

"Hm??"

Her green eyes narrowed.

"I do not know any Ludmilla."

"Why weren't you at the Fun Fair?" Jack said.

"What Fun Fair?"

"Hampstead."

"I live in Chelsea."

"DON'T LIE TO ME!!"

Jack leaned over. He must have been flailing because boxes and prints were all over the ground.

"GOD DID NOT DESTROY JOB!" he shouted. "BUT THEN HE NEVER SENT YOU!!"

She backed away.

"What's the matter?" Jack said. "Does God-talk bother you?"

"Not usually."

She was gone.

"O! O!"

A fist punched Jack in the face.

"THAT'S MY STALL!"

An arm knocked him into a black iron fence. Jack butted. A face spurted blood.

"That stall was meant for me!" Jack yelled.

The man chased Jack through billowing silks of the Sikhs, then went back to his prints. Jack slumped on a block. *In Memoriam John Law Barker formerly of the Madras Army born 1789*. An iron-bar roof covered steps leading down. PLEASE KEEP ROOF LOCKED AT ALL TIMES. The night market closed. Overhead was the black rear rosette window of the church. Green poles, empty and glistening, dripped. A tiny green wagon, its tongue on the ground, stood in a corner.

Black ate the tops of St. Martin's pillars.

Rivulets ran to Covent Garden. Jack followed. Columns, arcades and pediments brightened. An angel with a pocked face looked down. *Every Man Is a Debtor.* Stage hands removed Covent Gardens.

"O . . . stars."

Jack wiped his eyes.

"O."

A one-legged horse turned round and round, teeth bared.

A sweet thing is the Word of God.

A pomegranate tree bloomed in a charnel house. An old man in a dormer window smiled and put a finger to his lips.

Broken bits of lintels, pediments and columns rolled east under orange clouds with black holes. Four white bridges radiated from a domed cathedral. Red buses and pedestrians crossed those bridges. A black river looped to the sea spitting silver bubbles from silver eddies.

Jack stumbled.

"O."

Shoreditch market lighted up.

"O."

The roof projected on white struts. Electric crossbars ran through branches and leaves coming out of white stone. A white frieze ran over broken supports. Charred wood lay under black windows.

Inside, in the dark, an old Muslim, bearded and skinny, in a purple robe, swung a thin gold necklace.

"For your sweetheart?"

Turks and Persians crowded tables of power tools by a high chair, cabinet and a black typewriter on the sidewalk. Ginger lay on a pink blanket. Rusted files stuffed a wood box. Green night lights flared. Albanians, Serbs and Macedonians, their faces bright white, stood on Sclater Street. Croatians sold cigarettes from an open car boot. Sheets hung from a telephone booth. Russians and Poles sold glittering CDs.

A gold-red light rose over the flat steaming roofs of the East End.

"O."

Jack went down Brick Lane. It smelled of saffron. *Sutkar Vegetarian Restaurant. Serving Asian Disabled. Silk Sarees. Balti House.* Jack grabbed an aubergine from a vegetable cart. A Bangladeshi chased him.

"You must pay!"

The Bangladeshi caught him.

"Give it to me!"

"No!"

"*Surrender!*"

He snatched it back and walked away.

"Islam means *surrender*," he said.

Jack crawled on his hands and knees to Whitechapel Road.

"O, hunger . . ."

He came to a street sweeper.

"Are you an Imam?" Jack asked.

"No."

"But you must be."

"Why?"

"Who else could sweep such gold-red dust?"

"Maybe," the sweeper said. "But I am not an Imam."

Jack woke. A religious school let out. Young Muslim girls with red school bags came out under a Japanese maple whose leaves raised and lowered. Jack got up. There were strings and trails of strings on the pavement. Black leaked out of Angel Alley. Photographs of Miss Iraq lined a store window. Pakistanis celebrated a soccer win over Sri Lanka. Black dots floated. Headless people went by.

Across the road, the East London Mosque stood, orange brick, a cream-coloured minaret and copper dome. A muezzin cried over the East End. Gold-red light came from a chandelier.

> *Allah is the light of the heavens and the earth: the light is like a niche in which a lamp glows and the glass like a brilliant star lit from a blessed tree.*

Jack fell at the Jewish monument. A black iron *putto*

straddled a black iron spout. A black iron angel wore a Roman war helmet. At its feet was a black iron *putto*. A *putto* held an ark with a flag. Another held a concertina. *In Grateful and Loving Memory of Edward VII Rex et Imperator erected from subscriptions raised by Jewish inhabitants of east London*. A broken word, *ASILE*, stood where there should have been water but there was none. A black iron angel spread wings. It wore a radiated crown. *LIBERTY*.

"HUNGER!"

English men with big bellies went by. Englishmen pushed wheeled cages.

"CHRIST!" he shouted. "DON'T LET ME DIE HERE! I KNEW GOD! DIDN'T I? SOMEBODY, TELL ME I DID!"

A Hindu in a pink shirt drove a road sprinkler. He threw something at Jack. Jack lowered his head. It hit him in the chest. Inside was a styrofoam cup of tea and carrot cake wrapped in wax paper.

"FOOD!"

Jack grabbed the carrot cake.

"I clutch my moist white bag of carrot cake because I am hungry! I eat! It tastes good! Because I was HUNGRY!"

Jack wiped his eyes.

"I am so grateful. And look — a styrofoam cup of tea! ENGLISH TEA! WITH A TEA BAG!"

Jack sucked his fingers.

"YUM!!"

Jack walked Whitechapel.

"O. God is good. God bless God. God is very good to

me. I love God. God is a friend of mine."

Jack put his fingers under his arm pits and waved his elbows.

"BAWK! BAWK! BAWK!"

A Muslim waggled Jack's jaw.

"OW!"

"SPEAK OF GOD!"

Wind picked up. Guy wires twanged. Orange and white dust blew. Jack stood on the corner of Whitechapel and Brady Street. Hindu boys surged on bicycles past a Hebrew burial ground in a red-brick wall.

"Watch out!"

"Hey!"

"Stupid Englishman!"

"Sod off!"

An African-British woman in a tight black dress, with elaborate braids, came from a street market. She held a clipboard.

"Have you had a head injury?"

"Yes."

"It's for insurance purposes," she said. "People fall and sue the shopkeepers."

Jack pointed.

"I fell right there. By the Jewish monument. Right after I had reappeared."

"Sign here. And here is five pounds. Go have a lager at the *Grave Maurice*."

"Where?"

"Behind the street market.

Jack put the money in his pocket and walked into

the market. It was on the sidewalk and ran from Brady Street to the *Blind Beggar* on Cambridge Heath Road. Old Muslim men, dressed in robes, had conversations. Embroidered tablecloths lay on a folding chair. Andrex toilet paper leaned against the street rail. Model cars glittered, a table of clocks ticked, chained luggage lay by zebra fabric, cradles and spectacles in a box. Children's jumpers hung from a white van's open door. Cellophane blew. *Ravaya* and *kudu* were sold, *tahea*, onions and green mangoes. Muslim boys went by eating sweets. A green balance scale stood on a green cart with a box of tiny weights.

An Iraqi boy swung on a pole.

"Turkey figs!"

Pink blossoms fell. Muslim girls walked by in red silk blouses and gold and green shawls.

"Spanish dates!"

"Hot spice gingerbread!"

"Fresh and sweet!"

Pink candy floss hung from a wire. Plastic umbrellas were filled with red and yellow candy hearts.

"Cherries on the bough!"

"Velvet and silk!"

The *Grave Maurice* was a flat-walled pub in a wall of shops at the sidewalk of the market. Its door was unpainted. It was warm wood. A shirtless Brit stood in front of the *Grave Maurice*.

"Hey, mate," Jack said. "You're indecent."

"Sod off."

Jack went in.

"Ah. The English."

The *Grave Maurice* had an old hardwood floor. Brown varnished tables stood with wood rails instead of legs. The counter was yellow and projected with brown slats. It had a black border. A post went to a pale yellow ceiling that had black rafters. Beer kegs stood on a shelf with a clock. Beer cards hung like pennants. NO TRAVELLERS. English men stared at the clock. Dual faces split apart. Union Jacks drooped. A man drank, heel on the bar rail, eyes up toward the ceiling.

"I've seen terrible things," he said.

Jack bought a pint of Fosters and sat at a window table. Dirty lace hung at the lower half, at the street market. Inside the pub, a toddler reached to the counter. Two billiard tables stood under three lights by a grey upholstered bench. A thin black cord curved to a television set on a high shelf. A bicycle leaned against a wall.

"Publican!" Jack said. "The beer is off!"

"It can't be off."

"It's Fosters."

The publican's arm elongated across the floor, took Jack's glass and returned with a new full glass.

"Cheers."

The African-Briton woman with braided hair and a clipboard went by. Men pounded tables.

"Hoo! Hoo!"

Jack counted his change.

"Six pence, six pence, a shilling . . ."

"We don't use shillings any more," the publican said

An Australian came in on a crutch. He wore a wide-brimmed hat. Suddenly he kicked high. Jack ducked.

"Look at my feet! Not my eyes!"

At the hour of your death you will know what to do.

A large-boned woman with dyed auburn hair drank at the bar in a row of men. She brushed her hair back.

"Whitechapel isn't Whitechapel no more," she said. "Where is the East End? I look for it. I do not find it. In the name of God, where is it? I ask you, where is it?"

Jack stood.

"And now," he said. "Jack Russell will dance an Irish jig."

He danced.

"Without music!"

He sat.

"O, Lord," the auburn-haired woman said. "They kicked the Jews out, too. Lovely people. I worked for them. Very kind."

"It's a government scam," a man said.

"Winds me up."

"Me, too," Jack said.

"You know what I am saying," she said.

"I do."

"Do you? Do you? I don't believe you."

"Well, I do."

Jack drank.

"The squire jumps from bough to bough," he said.

Hindu girls passed by. One wore a blue sari with a gold and red shawl. The other wore a green sari with silver trim.

"What should we do?" the auburn-haired woman said.

"You know," a man said.

"What?"

"Well."

"Specifically."

"I'm just saying."

The door to the gentlemen's room opened and creaked shut.

"Look at the Muslim children," the woman said. "Are these people hateful? Can they be? With children like these? It cannot be. Not with those beautiful children."

"Dolls walk the enchanted road," Jack said.

Jack stood. He threw Fosters into the air.

"IT WAS HORRIBLE!!"

The publican came.

"AWFUL!!"

"Conduct yourself."

"Sod off!"

Jack punched the publican. The publican grabbed his hand. Jack shook it free and kicked. The publican threw him into a wall. Billiard balls clacked. Jack slid down.

"YOU THREW HIM TOO HARD!"

It was night.

"You'd like to slip into something comfortable, wouldn't you?" the auburn-haired woman was saying, "Yeah? Well, leave me alone."

Men cackled.

"O, you bad girl!"

The market was over. Black handbags and a pair of shoes lay in a gutter. A Hindu pushed a four-poster bed and a boy folded blue plastic bags into wood boxes. The *Blind Beggar* lighted up. Purple clouds rolled to a black canal. A blue heron walked a feeder canal. A black lizard rolled dice. Its eyes were ochre. Pink rain fell. A peacock mounted a muskrat. They fused into a seal with blue feathers. Light flickered over the eastern marshes. Wild grass moved in clanging swells.

Sweet England docked.

FSC
www.fsc.org
RECYCLED
Paper made from
recycled material
FSC® C005834